TAKEN

Book Three of the Keeper Chronicles

BEN MEEKS

Sidestreet
Publishing LLC

THE KEEPER CHRONICLES

Petrified

Betrayal

Taken

CHAPTER • 1

Sweat rolled off my forehead and into my eyes. I wiped it away and refocused on the task at hand. I held up the diagram, getting a closer look at my next step. I had been working on the assembly for the better part of an hour. Now I was at a critical juncture. If I didn't get this connection right, then I would have a disaster on my hands. I pushed the diagram away and picked up a bottle of cyanoacrylate. Once the adhesive was applied, I would be on the clock. I applied a thin strip and put the bottle back on the table. I exhaled half my breath and held the rest to steady my hands like a sniper preparing for a shot. I only had a few seconds to make the connection. As carefully as I could I brought the pieces together.

Just as they touched, I was startled by a buzzing in my pocket. I'd been so focused I nearly jumped out of my skin. I exhaled and looked at my work, it was a mess. I sighed out the breath I'd been holding as my phone buzzed again. I took it out and checked the screen, the caller ID said Restricted.

I put the phone to my ear. "Hello?"

The voice on the other end sounded like it was being put through one of those scramblers you see on television. "A demon is on its way to Dave Hutchinson. He'll be dead by midnight. If you hurry you can help him."

"Who is this?" I asked.

"A friend," the voice said. "I'll send you the address."

The call ended. I sat back in my chair, pondering the brief conversation. I'd never heard of Dave Hutchinson. I'd thought I'd put an end to the summoning, at least for the time being, when I'd gotten the Grimoire from Harlan. My phone buzzed again. I'd received a text from a restricted number with an address. I wasn't sure if the lead was credible, but it was less than an hour away. Seemed worth checking out.

"Holt," I shouted.

I could hear the thumping of his footsteps leave his room and walk down the hallway to where I was. He walked as if he had lead soled shoes. The footsteps stopped and the door opened.

Holt stuck in his head. "By the mother, why's it so hot in here?"

"I got a te—"

"I mean, even though winter's over, it's still been chilly but you keep tellin' me not to turn the thermostat over sixty-six, and I do it, 'cause I'm a pleasure to live with, but I'm walkin' around here freezin' my ass off and you got a space heater keeping your room a toasty fifteen hundred degrees. I'm just curious—" He stopped talking long enough to see what I was doing. "Oh no, not this again."

I scratched my chin and ran a hand over my face.

"Obie . . . this ain't healthy. We're supposed to be Keepers of the Earth Mother for fucks sake. Name takers and demon slayers," he said. "She's been gone what four or five months already and you hadn't done nothin' but sit around and mope and build these dump planes."

It had been four months and seventeen days since Naylet left on her trip of self-discovery, not that I was counting, I just hadn't been able to get the running tally out of my head. It seemed like since Naylet had left I couldn't stop thinking about her. Wondering where she was and what she was doing. I could probably find out if I wanted to; the wererats information network was vast, to say the least. I had no doubt Adan could, and would, use it to keep tabs on her if I asked him. I promised myself I wouldn't and I hadn't needed to, the postcards I'd been getting gave me a good idea of what she was up to.

"There's nothing wrong with assembling transportation collectibles," I said.

He put his hands on his hips and shook his head. "Do you hear yourself right now? Transportation collectibles? You know they do therapy online . . . It'll be real easy to find someone to talk to."

I was losing my patience with him. "Why. Are. You. Here?"

"How the hell should I know, you called me," Holt said.

"Right," I sighed. "I just got an anonymous lead that says a guy is going to be attacked by a demon. I figured we'd check it out."

"Hell yeah," Holt said. "It'll be good for you to get back to work."

"Give me five minutes and we'll go. And close the door behind you."

I looked back at the P-51 Mustang I had been working on. I'd been trying to glue the fuselage together. The pieces weren't on straight. I could pull it off and try it again but not without leaving marks on the plastic. Maybe I could add some bullet holes to cover up the imperfections. Or maybe Holt was right. I wouldn't tell him that, of course, but it might do me some good to get out of my head a little. I put the plane down on my worktable, turned off the heater, and rubbed my eyes. I wasn't sure how solid the lead was, but it would do me good to get out of the house.

When I made it outside, I found Holt behind the wheel of his Honda. After I'd discovered how good he was behind the wheel I always let him drive.

"You think Adan could find out who sent you that message?" Holt asked a few minutes down the road. "The wererats are good at finding out stuff like that."

"They're great if you're not in a hurry. It could take them a month to get back to us with something like that. By then we will have either figured it out ourselves or it won't matter anymore."

Holt shrugged. "Suit yourself. I don't see what it would hurt to get the ball rolling on it."

"When you're out on your own you'll have the luxury and responsibility of making the decision. As long as you're my apprentice just enjoy not having to make the hard decisions."

We rode in silence until we were close to our destination. I could see the blue and red lights flashing from the road before we pulled into the subdivision.

"Looks like we're too late," Holt said.

"Let's go in for a look anyway."

A couple firetrucks, an ambulance, and more than a few police cars were parked in front of the house.

"What now?" Holt asked.

"Just pull through," I said. "Let's see what we can see."

Holt drove slowly down the center of the street toward the lights. An officer waved us through. I couldn't see anything from the street and getting inside right now wasn't going to be an option. I was starting to think we'd have to come back the next day when things had calmed down when I spotted Detective Farwell standing in the yard. We'd met the day Naylet was turned to stone. I'd saved him from the same fate and in the process exposed him to our world. He wasn't my biggest fan . . . what an ingrate.

"Pull over up here," I said waving a finger at the road ahead. "I got an idea."

Holt took the next right beside a two-story brick house and parked up the street. I got out and walked to the corner in view of the house. Farwell talked to a woman wearing dark blue coveralls with a laminated badge hanging from her right chest pocket. Probably the medical examiner. I pulled my phone out of my pocket and gave him a call. I watched him fish the phone out of his pocket and stared at the screen as it rang. He looked at it for three rings before he shoved it back in his pocket and returned his attention to the woman.

I typed out a text message. *Brick house on the corner. Need to talk to you.*

Farwell glanced at his phone again, mouthed the word *Shit,* and looked down the street in my direction. When he spotted me, I put two fingers to my forehead and gave him a casual salute. He ducked the police tape and walked over to meet me on the corner.

"What the hell are you doing here?" he asked.

"I got a call that there was something going on here in my area of expertise. What happened?"

Farwell crossed his arms. "It's an ongoing investigation."

"Look, if you tell me this has nothing to do with the kinds of things I handle then I'll be more than happy to head home and leave you to it. If you think this might be . . . something else, then you know better than anyone the kind of danger you and your officers could be in without my help. Your call."

Farwell wrapped his tongue over his top teeth and sucked on them as he turned back to look at the house. "Alright. We found a man and woman handcuffed to chairs in the bedroom. The coroner said they were missing organs but she wouldn't know exactly how bad it was until she got them back for an autopsy."

"So, they had some organs harvested? Like black market, leave you in a bathtub full of ice, kind of thing?" I asked.

"Well, that's the kicker, there weren't any incisions. The bodies were in great shape, besides the missing organs," Farwell said. "The bodies are just . . . empty. What about you? What brought you out here?"

"I got an anonymous call that said there was demon stuff happening here. I guess I was too late to save Dave and his wife but I'll look into it."

"That's the thing. Mr. Hutchinson isn't here," Farwell said with a smirk. "The man we have is his business partner. It looks like he was giving it to Dave's wife on the side and they got caught. I was about to send a couple marked units to his construction site, see if we can pick him up."

"How about you give me the address and an hour head start?" I asked.

"Why would I do that?"

"I'm assuming the officers you send like their organs."

CHAPTER · 2

I became aware I hadn't been paying attention. I glanced at the clock: 11:47. Holt was talking, which wasn't unusual for him. Assuming he'd been going the whole ride it meant he'd been droning on for over thirty minutes and I had been lost in thought the whole time.

"You see, it's a problem because it was unnecessary to begin with and it completely changed Han's character," Holt said. "He was a dangerous rogue and now he looks passive and weak, like he has a moral code that wasn't there in the original version."

"Mm hmm," I said absently. "I can see you feel strongly about this."

"Strong enough to give you a tee shirt about it when we first met." Holt waved a hand in the air to accentuate his point. "And what about Greedo? He went from a competent bounty hunter who Han got the drop on to a chump that couldn't hit someone three feet in front of him. Since he's the only Rodian we see in any of the movies, even one through three, which I try not to think about, it makes the whole species look incompetent."

"It's really not fair," I said and pointed ahead on the left. "It should be right up here."

Holt slowed as we came up to a construction site. The land had been cleared, leaving a wasteland of red clay. Heavy machinery sat quietly around a muddy square of barren earth. Holt pulled the truck into the site and killed the lights. Being close to midnight, all the workers were long gone, or they should have been.

"Looks like we found him," Holt said, motioning toward the foreman's trailer on the edge of the property.

Slivers of light escaped around the curtains hanging in the window. We pulled around and found a white truck parked in front. Holt and I got out and walked up on either side of the truck. In the back was a toolbox mounted behind the cab, some five-gallon buckets, and a couple suitcases. The cab had an assortment of trash filling up the passenger floorboard. Everything from fast food wrappers to beer cans. A little movement and extra light from the trailer got my attention. Blinds collapsed back together. We had lost the element of surprise. We walked up a ramp to the front door.

I knocked. "Dave Hutchinson, can you open the door please?"

"You sound like a cop," Holt chuckled.

I held up a finger over my lips.

Dave replied, "The site's closed. Make an appointment with my secretary."

"I need to talk to you about your wife," I said.

It was quiet for a second before Dave said, "What about her?"

"I'd rather speak face to face."

We waited. There was no reply, no footsteps, just silence.

"He's ignoring us," Holt said, sounding genuinely surprised.

"Yeah, it happens more than you think," I said. "I've found the best thing to do—"

Holt punched the door leaving a fist imprint. "Open the damn door, numb nuts!"

"...is not that," I sighed.

That's when the chanting started and I realized that Dave wasn't a hapless victim, he was our villain with two murders under his belt. The time for talk had passed. If we didn't get in fast, we'd have another demon on our hands.

I opened the Velcro I added to all my pants to make room for my large muscular tail, kicked off my shoes, and made the change to krasis, my half animal half human form. I grew fur over my body with the head of an otter, paws instead of feet, clawed fingers on my hands, and of course the tail. The shifter blade that resided in my body in my other forms came out. It was in a leather sheath that held it to my back, the handle by my waist with the tip by my left shoulder. It was the only configuration I had found that was comfortable to wear and didn't destroy my clothes through the change.

Holt followed my lead and made the change to krasis, taking on the aspect of a Doberman. He stood seven feet tall, with the head, fur, and paws of a dog. He clenched his hands around the knuckledusters in his hands, his weapon of choice.

Holt tried the door. "It's locked."

"Watch out."

He moved to the side. I stepped back and delivered a kick that should have popped the door right open. Instead, it only moved about an inch and left me with a twinge in my ankle.

"He barricaded the door," I said.

I shook my foot out as Holt threw his body against the door. It opened a little more each time he collided with it. By the third hit the door was open a few inches and the chanting inside stopped. I could suddenly smell rotting meat wafting from inside the trailer. A second later it sounded like the foreman was choking.

"What do you see?" I asked.

Holt moved his head around trying to get a look inside. "Nothing, too much shit in the way."

I stepped up beside Holt. "Together this time."

The door shifted in a couple more inches on the bottom and collapsed in on the top and the barricade crashed down. I gave the door a final push and got it open enough to slide inside. I drew my blade and climbed over the pile of furniture into the trailer with Holt right behind me.

The foreman lay on the floor with blood running out of his mouth, nose, and ears. I couldn't tell what killed him but judging from the amount of blood, it wasn't an easy way to go. A cloth with a summoning circle drawn on it was spread out on the floor beside the body. A small cardboard box had been knocked over spilling gray powder onto the carpet.

I knew what it was right away, dust. The processed remains of ultra-natural creatures like me. It was the power source for magic. Holt pulled a crumpled bag out of the box and scooped as much of the dust into it as he could. Since the processing facility Hob ran had been destroyed, dust was in high demand.

"Where is it?" He asked, shoving the bag into his pocket.

The desk chairs and filing cabinets had been pushed in front of the door to form the barricade with everything else from papers to a stapler to a houseplant thrown on top.

I scanned the pile. "Not sure. Stay alert."

The last thing I wanted was to get jumped by a demon trying to suck my brain out . . . again. I kept my blade in front of me and backed against the wall. I looked around the room. I didn't see anything in the furniture pile and the rest of the room was empty except for some strewn papers and the dead foreman. No bloodthirsty demons.

I scratched my head. "There's nothing here."

"You don't think it went back through the portal do you?" Holt asked.

"If it did, then who opened it?"

He shrugged. "Maybe it's a smart demon? It opened its own portal?"

It was a possibility. It wouldn't be the first time a demon took advantage of some poor sap and skipped town, leaving us to clean up the mess. No demon meant there wasn't anything for us to do but gather up any evidence of the occult. I'd give Farwell a heads-up once we were out of the way.

"There's a piece of paper under the body," Holt said.

I put my blade back in its sheath. "What is it?"

Holt took the corner of the paper, pulled it out, and passed it to me. It was stained with the foreman's blood. I didn't bother trying to keep the blood off my hands, it was a little late for that. It was a letter with a summoning ritual on it. Unlike most rituals I run across, it was a print-out, rather than handwritten, complete with step-by-step instructions and phonetic notations for the incantation.

"Let me see that box," I said.

Holt passed it to me. The return address was from a P.O. box in Oklahoma. I ripped off the address label and shoved it in my pocket with the letter.

"There's something weird with the body," Holt said. "There's a bulge in his belly, some kind of swelling or something."

He poked the body. The body shifted from the pressure. The swelling in the abdomen rippled.

"Obie . . ."

"I see it," I said, dropping the box and drawing my blade.

The rippling turned into a wave that rushed up the throat. A monster resembling a giant centipede shot out of the mouth at Holt. Holt fell back, grabbing the demon with both hands. The demon's jaws snapped as its body began to wrap around Holt's arm. I was able to get a swing in before the two of them became intertwined. My blade cut cleanly through it. It screeched, the top part of its body lashing wildly as its bottom part fell to the floor, still running down the corpse's throat.

"You got it?" I asked.

Holt held the thrashing beast at arm's length. "Yeah, what do we do with it now?"

"There's some buckets in the back of that truck," I said. "Hang onto it."

I climbed over the barricade and went outside. I grabbed a half full bucket of joint compound out of the back of the truck and dashed back inside. I ripped the lid off and used my hand to scoop what I could onto the floor.

I put the bucket in front of Holt and grabbed the lid. "Toss it in!"

"It's holding onto my arm," he said. "Hang on."

He slammed it down on the desk with a crunch. The demon shuddered, stunned from the impact. Holt threw the demon into the bucket as if spiking a football. I slammed the lid on top. No sooner had I snapped it into place than the bucket began to shake. I could see the shadow of the demon as it thrashed around inside the bucket.

"Uh . . . Obie," Holt said. "Where'd the rest of it go?"

I looked at the body. There had been two feet of demon centipede sticking out of Dave's mouth. His head had fallen to the side, his mouth open wide in a silent scream. The demon was missing.

"Stay quiet," I said.

I listened, but all I could hear was the thumping coming from the bucket. Holt moved around to the desk. A second centipede, presumably made from cutting the first, shot out and scurried up Holt's leg. He screamed and spun, trying to grab it, but it was too quick. It had already bit him on the neck before he could get a hand on it. He pulled it away with bits of his flesh in its jaws. Blood soaked into his shirt.

"Put it on the floor," I shouted.

He slammed it down on its back and held it in place. "You ain't going to cut it again are ya?"

"Nope."

I put a foot on top of the bucket to keep the other demon from getting out and stretched. It felt like a game of Twister. I held the demon still with one hand and with the other I lined the blade up with the center of its body. With a sudden stab, I drove the blade through its body and into the floor. It let out a high pitched squeal as it thrashed in pain. We had it pinned, it wasn't going anywhere for the time being.

"Hold this one," I said, pointing to the bucket.

Holt put a hand on it.

"Yell if they get loose," I said.

"You can count on it."

I climbed over the barricade and out the door. I grabbed another bucket from the back of the truck. When I made it back inside the trailer, I found Holt sitting on the bucket with the trapped demon. The second demon thrashed on the floor.

I pulled the top off the bucket and scooped it out as fast as I could. "Get that thing ready to move."

I put a foot on the bucket when Holt stood up. He knelt over the demon and flexed his right hand around the knuckleduster. He grabbed the demon with his left hand to hold it still and drove his weaponized fist down on its head. The first strike resulted in a stomach turning crunch. The second strike had less crunch and more splatter as the creature's head ruptured, spilling green ooze out onto the desk. The demon went limp.

"You think we killed it?" Holt asked.

I pulled my blade out of the floor. "Let's not risk it."

I grabbed it and tossed it in the bucket. I snapped the lid in place and put the buckets a few feet apart.

"Grab the desk," I said.

Holt cleared the desk and picked it up. "What are we doing with it?"

"Set it on top."

He flipped it over and placed it on the buckets. With the desk out of the way we were able to open the door and walk outside.

"Let's see that bag of dust," I said.

Holt pulled the bag out of his pocket. "What are we doin' with it?"

"We'll burn 'em."

Holt pulled the dust back from my outstretched hand. "Are you sure, this stuff's in short supply. It's worth a lotta money."

"Can you think of another option? Unless you got a full can of gas in your back pocket."

"Fair enough," he said. "Can I do it? I've never done it before."

"It's the only dust we have," I said. "Next time, okay?"

"Come on, how hard can it be? I've seen Livy light her fireplace a bunch a times. Same thing, right?"

I wasn't thrilled about the idea, but I was supposed to be teaching him and it would be good practice with minimal risk. "Alright, but be careful."

"Sweet," he said, moving in front of the door. "What do I do?"

"When you're ready, open the bag. Imagine fire in your mind. Throw the dust and ignite it."

He seemed hesitant. "How do I ignite it?"

"Imagine it catching fire. Livy says the word to help focus the intent. Folks like Hob don't have to do that anymore."

"Got it, he said.

He took the bag out, stood perfectly still for a second before tossing it in and shouting, "Fire!"

Flames erupted inside the trailer with enough force to send the window flying into the front of my truck. Flames roared through the open door and engulfed half of Holt. I dove to the ground.

"You alright?" I asked, picking myself up.

The air was heavy with the scent of burning hair.

"Yeah, just a little singed."

I headed for the truck. "Let's get out of here quick."

The flames were pouring out of the windows by the time Holt pulled onto the pavement.

"Where to?" Holt asked.

"We need to find out who's sending summoning rituals by mail."

"Kinda hard to do in the middle of the night," he said.

"We'll go home and take care of it after the sun comes up."

"I've got that job I've been looking into," Holt said. "You need me or can I work on my own thing."

Finding leads was a big part of being a Keeper. I'd had Holt start looking into some on his own. They had all turned into a dead-end, except one. That wasn't unusual, most leads turned out to be nothing. I was glad to see him getting involved in the work, taking a little initiative. I didn't want to discourage him and I didn't really need him to ask around about a letter.

"Sure," I said. "Don't engage anything without me, okay?"

"You got it."

CHAPTER · 3

The problem I had was, anyone who knew about someone selling summoning rituals wouldn't be in my circles. If they were, they definitely wouldn't tell me about it. There was only one person I could think of that had an outside chance of knowing: a local hunter. *Wannabe hunter* might be more accurate. Travis was a nice guy, but wholly unsophisticated. To the best of my knowledge he had never actually caught or killed an ultranatural. That's probably why everyone tolerated him the way we did.

I would've liked to call him, but didn't have his number. Hell, I wasn't sure he even had a phone. I found his house, a run-down shack in the woods. It was well kept, but old and needed work that I got the impression Travis couldn't afford. A roughly thirty-year-old pickup was parked out front. I think it had been red when it was new but after decades in the rain and sun had faded into pink. I parked my truck beside it and got out. The sun was just coming up. I hated to show up so early but I needed answers.

I didn't make it onto the porch before Travis came out to greet me. "Well I'll be," he said, putting his hands on his hips. "Ain't this a surprise."

I smiled. "Hey, Travis, sorry to show up so early on a Sunday."

His black hair was buzzed short. He had a rather nice white button-up shirt under his usual dingy pair of overalls. He wasn't wearing any shoes.

I stuck my keys in my pocket. "You heading to church?"

"Naw, why do ya ask?"

"You're all dressed up. That's a nice shirt," I said.

Travis looked a little uncomfortable. "Oh, yeah, I found 'er at the Goodwill and was just tryin' her on."

"I didn't mean to interrupt. Is now a bad time?"

"Naw, not at all. Sit right here and I'll grab us a drink," he said. "I don't get visitors often. I got a couple beers, or some soda pop, what'll ya have."

"A little early for a beer ain't it?" I asked.

"It's five o'clock somewhere." He grinned. "You ain't gonna let me drink alone, is ya?"

I shrugged. "Just some water then."

Travis disappeared inside and returned a few minutes later wearing one of his normal ragged old tees under his overalls. He was carrying a dingy looking glass full of even dingier looking water in one hand and a Bud Light in the other. The water had a slight orange tint and smelled like rotten eggs. If I had smelled it under different circumstances I'd think I would have a demon to hunt. Here, it was just well water that needed a good filtration and softening system. We took a seat in rocking chairs at the end of the porch.

"Thanks," I said, taking the glass.

Even if I was thirsty, I wouldn't want to take a sip, but I decided to hold onto the glass long enough not to offend him.

"What can I do for ya, Obie?"

"I don't really know how to get into it, but you told me you were into cryptozoology . . . I have some questions."

He choked in the middle of a swig. He coughed, trying to catch his breath. Beer ran down his chin. "What'd ya see? A fairy? Werewolf? Were it Bigfoot?"

"Oh no, nothing like that," I said. "The truth is, I had a friend who's gotten into that occult stuff. I'm worried about him and thought with your experience you might be able to give me some direction."

"Let's be clear, Obie. The occult's 'nother can a worms," Travis said. "Take ya average sasquatch or leprechaun. They don't really mean no harm to nobody. They's just animals. You leave them alone and they leave you alone . . . for the most part. We ain't talking about them Wiccan's neither. They ain't Christian, don't get me wrong, but they ain't all bad. Occult is something different. Dark magic, sacrifices, baby killers and demon worshipers. People with evil in they's heart." Travis put his beer down on the porch and leaned forward for emphasis. "Obie, you get your friend away from that stuff. There ain't nothin' good that's gonna come from it."

"I'm trying," I said. "Do you have any idea where someone could get stuff like that? It came through the mail. Have you heard of anything like this before?" I pulled the shipping label out of my pocket and handed it to him.

Travis took the label, gave it a side eye, and passed it back. "I don't mess with the occult, except maybe with a scattergun, and I ain't too good on the internet neither."

I took out the letter and opened it. It was mostly dry. I was raised better than to hand people bloody letters, so I laid it out on a little table between the rocking chairs.

Travis leaned over for a closer look. "Is that blood?"

"I said I *had* a friend."

"Dagburn, Obie. What you got into?"

"It's a mess, I know," I said.

"I'll be right back."

When he went inside, I took the glass of water and dumped some over the side of the porch and then pressed my lip against the edge of the glass to make it look like I had taken a drink. I waited, holding it close to my mouth. When he came back outside, I put it back on the table.

"I was lookin' for a card I had. Some feller came by about a year ago. He said they was a place on the computer that I could go to order all kinds of stuff. Weapons, some kind of magic powder, even locations of monsters to hunt if I wanted. He said it was some special dark place on the internet and I could buy anything I wanted with some cryptic money. I ain't too good on the computer, and I ain't sitting too high on the hog, so I never done nothing with it. Could be that your friend got a card, too."

"How have I not heard of this?" I said more to myself than to Travis.

Travis sat back in the rocking chair. "Because you ain't a part of that world. I know you and Hank think I'm nuts, but I'm telling you, hand to God, they's some nasty things out there."

I had to talk to Travis for another twenty minutes before I was able to get away. My phone rang just as I got to the truck. It was Holt.

"Are you done?" Holt asked.

"Kind of hit a dead end. I should be home in about thirty minutes," I said.

"I'll be there as soon as I can. I'm about to finish up that job I was working on."

"Right now?" I asked.

I heard some leaves crunching through the phone.

"Yeah, I shouldn't be long."

"You were supposed to run it by me before you did anything," I said.

"Yeah, well, it's not what I thought, but something I need to handle," he said. "It's time sensitive."

"Alright, send me the address. And don't do anything until I get there."

"Can't promise that but I'll try," Holt said.

The address came through a moment later. I got there as fast as I could. Holt's car was parked on the side of the road. I pulled in behind him and followed his scent west into the woods. I hadn't gone far before Holt, in the form of a Doberman, came bounding up from my left. He stopped in front of me and motioned with his head in the direction he had come from. I followed him the rest of the way to a trailer. It was wholly unremarkable. Nothing about it stood out, the kind of place you forget two minutes after you see it. We stopped on the edge of the tree line and Holt made the change to krasis.

"You really didn't have to come," he said. "I can handle this one myself."

I changed to krasis and drew my blade. "Maybe, but I'm here and there's no reason to risk a fight alone."

Holt looked worried. He wasn't acting like his normal gung-ho self. "Alright, what do we do?"

"It's your hunt, I'll follow your lead," I said.

"Alright, there should only be one guy in the house we're worried about," he said. "We'll go in the back."

I followed Holt around to the back of the house and up a little porch to the door. He tried the handle. It wasn't locked. We stepped inside into a hallway. The house was quiet. The flicker of a screen in a room at the end of the hall caught my attention. Holt motioned for me to check the left side of the house while he went toward the light. I followed the hallway into a kitchen. The living room was beside it with a door on the far wall. I walked over to the door and listened. I didn't hear anything, so I opened it a crack. It looked like a spare bedroom. I heard a crash from the other side of the trailer.

I ran back to find Holt standing over a man. The man's forehead was dented from the impact of Holt's knuckledusters. Blood ran from his ears. He wasn't dead. His chest rose and fell lightly. I had no doubt he would die shortly without help.

"I'm not smelling any demons," I said. "I guess we got lucky. This one was easy. Let's find any magic stuff or dust he has and get outta here."

"He doesn't have anything like that," Holt said.

"What do you mean?"

Holt looked me in the eye. "He's not summoning demons."

The man's chest stopped moving.

"Okay. It seems to me like we just broke in and killed a guy for no reason," I said. "What am I missing?"

Holt turned the computer monitor the man had been looking at so I could see it. It was pornography . . . of young boys. I looked at the man lying on the floor. I didn't feel the need to try and revive him. I wasn't sure how to handle this. It wasn't really in our jurisdiction. It made no difference to Thera, so we weren't obligated to police it.

"How did you find out about this guy?" I asked.

"By accident," he said. "I've been looking for people doing hinky shit. I found one." He pointed to a closet with a padlock on it. "You want to do the honors?"

I stuck my blade between the lock and the door and pried it off. The closet stunk and was empty except for a five-gallon bucket and a boy that looked to be about six years old. He cowered in the corner. He had his head buried in his arms and wouldn't look up at us. That was alright with me, I didn't want him to see us. I grabbed Holt's arm and pulled him down the hallway.

Holt held up his hands. "I know what you're thinking. It's true he wasn't summoning demons or whatever but he was hurting people . . . kids, and that's just as bad. You told me I have to decide the kind of Keeper I want to be. I'm the kind that isn't going to let a kid get hurt if I can help it."

"What about him?" I asked pointing at the corpse with my chin.

"Look, a couple months ago that lizard thing Slagtooth just about disemboweled me. As far as I'm concerned that thing's a demon. If I was you, I'd head over to the diving bell and cut its head off. That tells me there's some discretion in the decision making. I'm not going to apologize for doing what's right."

"No," I said. "I mean what are you going to do with the body."

Holt shrugged. "There's nothing really to do is there? I don't really want the kid to see him. Could he be 'sustainably sourced'?"

"Even the Tortured Occult won't eat a pedophile," I said. "Just leave him for the cops. We don't want them to waste time looking for him."

I grabbed a blanket off the bed and tossed it over the body. I took out my phone and called Detective Farwell. He would no doubt be thrilled to hear from me again so soon. It rang a few times. I was beginning to think I would have to leave a message when he finally answered.

"What the hell do you want now?" he said.

"That's no way to answer the phone."

"You're lucky I answered at all," Farwell said. "Are you watching me again? Which finger am I holding up?"

"I have an anonymous tip for you."

"It's not really anonymous if I know who you are is it?" he said.

I ignored his comment and continued. "I'm looking at a little boy that needs some help and a dead pedophile. I'm sure his parents are missing him. The kid, not the pedophile. Well, I guess his parents could be missing him too. I can't be sure."

"Is he safe?" Farwell asked.

"He's dead."

Farwell sighed. "No, the boy."

"I'll stay with him," Holt said.

"Yeah, he's safe. We'll keep an eye on him until you get here," I said. "You got a pen to write the address down?"

"Alright," he said. "Let me have it."

I relayed the address to him.

"One other thing," Farwell said. "If I find evidence that you murdered him, I will arrest you. No one's above the law."

I hung up the phone and turned to Holt. "I'll catch you up on everything later. Just meet me at the house when you're done here," I said.

"Should we be worried about Farwell?"

I gave him a smile. "No."

Holt took the form of a Doberman. I was curious so I stayed back and out of sight. After a few minutes Holt led the boy out of the trailer. They walked into the front yard and lay down beside each other. Just a boy and a dog waiting for the police.

CHAPTER • 4

I didn't know what Travis was talking about, but something told me Holt would have a better idea. He was more savvy with technology than I was. Hell, I'd only had a smartphone for less than a year now. I made it onto the front porch with my hand on the doorknob when I stopped short. I got that prickly feeling on the back of my neck I had come to trust. I turned to my right facing the woods. Everything seemed normal. I didn't see anyone sneaking through the trees. A brown thrasher landed on the porch railing, took a couple hops, and flew away. A cool breeze blew in from the west. I took a whiff of the air. I could smell petroleum products. The closest neighbor I had was a stone's throw through the trees in that direction. He did a lot of work on cars, rebuilding engines and oil changes. There was always some stench wafting over to my place.

I went to my room and sat at my desk. Holt would be a bit, I had some time to waste. I picked up the mangled P-51. It wasn't as bad as I'd originally thought. I could fix it.

Holt's words popped in my mind. *This ain't healthy.*

He was probably right. I didn't really give him credit for it, but for a goofball, he was surprisingly insightful. I pulled out my trashcan and dropped the plane into it. I ran an arm across the table, pushing the instructions and loose pieces into the can and put it back under my desk. Leaning back in the chair I let out a heavy sigh. My thoughts returned to Naylet. I picked up the stack of postcards Naylet had sent me. There were six so far being held together with a rubber band. I ran a thumb across the edge with enough pressure to make them flex and thump together as my thumb moved from one to the next. I tossed the cards on the desk. The models were a good distraction. I wasn't sure what I would do now. Maybe I should just finish the P-51. I'd already paid for it. I was reaching for the trashcan when my phone buzzed. I fished it out and looked at the screen. It was a restricted number . . . again.

I put it on speaker but didn't say anything right away. I wasn't sure what to say. I didn't know anything about this person. Maybe it was paranoia but I couldn't escape the feeling that whoever it was had an ulterior motive.

Finally, I spoke. "Yeah."

The scrambled voice said, "You weren't able to save Dave?"

"I wasn't given the whole story."

I could hear the smile as the person spoke. "Want to try again?"

"I want you to cut the crap."

"I assume you're aware of the disappearances?"

There had been a number of disappearances lately. I didn't know exactly how many. It seemed like every couple weeks, I'd get a call that someone didn't come home or didn't show up to work. I'd checked it out but never turned up anything. It's like they just vanished. Dishes in the sink and clothes in the wash, it was strange for sure. Sometimes ultranaturals don't put down roots in an area and move on after a bit. It makes it hard to know if someone's disappeared or just left. It's rare for them to leave all their belongings in place when they go but it isn't unheard of. There isn't exactly a national phone directory I can look them up in.

"Eddie, a forest troll you know, is next on the list. You might be able to save him, if you hurry."

"Who the hell is this?"

He hung up. I couldn't help but feel like I was being sent on a wild goose chase. Eddie had been doing some work for Hank, remodeling part of the clubhouse. Maybe he could give me an idea if Eddie was all right.

When Hank answered the phone, I asked, "You seen Eddie today?"

"No, he was supposed to do some work for me, but he didn't show up. Everything alright?"

"Send me his address and I'll let you know," I said.

"Yep."

I sat there wondering if I was actually going to go as the address came through. I didn't like being jerked around but I didn't really have anything else to go on. If I didn't show and Eddie got hurt that would be on me. I had no choice when it came down to it. I made it outside to see Holt pulling up.

He opened door of his Civic and got halfway out. "You good?"

I tossed him the key to my truck which he caught in his left hand. "I got another anonymous tip. Sounds like Eddie's in trouble."

I got in the passenger seat of my truck and pulled up the directions.

"How far is it?" he asked.

"Fifteen minutes. Listen, I've got some questions for you."

Holt cranked the engine and backed out. "I know what you're going to say. I know it wasn't demon stuff, but I wasn't going to let some kid get . . . I wasn't going to let him get any more hurt than he already was."

"No, I don't have a problem with that at all." I plugged my phone into the truck to display the directions for him. "You have to figure out what kind of Keeper you're going to be. Most Keepers would have just called it into the police. Some would have ignored it. Looks like you're the kind that will help a kid if you find one in trouble. Not everyone's like that. The truth is, I'm proud of you."

"Let's not make a big deal about it. Just doing my job," Holt said.

"Fair enough," I said. "I wanted to ask you about some things Travis told me about. It doesn't make any sense to me but you're more up to speed on technology."

Holt chuckled. "Ya think."

I ignored him. "He mentioned a dark place on the internet. Does that mean anything to you?"

"He was probably talking about the dark web. I don't really know anything about it other than people do a lot of illegal shit there."

"Okay, what about *cryptic currency?*" I asked, making air quotes with my fingers.

"Cryptocurrency." Holt nodded. "It's digital currency. That makes sense, I've heard people use cryptocurrency to buy things on the dark web. I'm no expert though."

"Alright, first things first, we'll check on Eddie and then figure out this dark web stuff."

CHAPTER • 5

We drove to the address Hank supplied. It was a rundown trailer set back about thirty feet from the road. There wasn't a clearly defined yard, there wasn't even any grass. It was as if someone cleared the trees, put a trailer in, and forgot about it. The whole place looked like a dump. There was a pickup truck with flat tires parked beside the trailer with thirty or forty bags of trash in the back. A rusted-out Oldsmobile, that looked like it might still run, was parked beside it. Holt pulled the truck in behind the Olds and we got out. The trailer was surrounded by what I would consider trash. Rusted grills, a few lawn mowers, a filing cabinet toppled over on top of a koi pond that was half full of green algae. That was just the nicer stuff. It would take a couple dumpsters and a week of work to get this place cleaned up. The door to the trailer was open. That wasn't something to be concerned about. A lot of poorer folks around here would open the doors and windows when the weather was nice. Being a couple weeks out of winter the weather was still cold but trolls tended to like it that way.

"What do ya think?" I asked.

"Well," Holt said, looking around. "I'd say we should look for signs of a struggle but how would we know?"

A frog jumped into the koi pond from a patch of weeds. I walked toward the front door. "Let's check inside."

We followed a trail that wound its way through the debris in the yard to the front door. I leaned in and gave the air a couple sniffs. The house smelled like mildew and troll.

Eddie was a regular at the clubhouse, but he wasn't in the T.O. He liked to hang around and play pool. I'd played him a few times over the years and I lost every time. I'd never been to his house before but it was about what I'd expect from a troll.

"Eddie," I shouted, leaning in the doorway. "You home?"

"You ain't worried about alerting the abductors?" Holt asked.

"I've got you watching my back."

I stepped into the living room. There was a couch with a flower print that looked as if it had been pulled out of a catalog from the seventies. A well-worn coffee table and modest tv were the only other adornments in the room.

"You smell that?" Holt asked.

I could smell something that reminded me of road construction. It reminded me of what I'd smelled on my front porch. "Yeah, stay alert."

The kitchen was off to the right with a hallway to the left. I walked into the kitchen and stuck my head into what turned out to be a laundry room. The kitchen had a few dirty dishes in the sink with a trail of ants scavenging the food remnants.

Holt looked at the ants and shook his head. "I feel sorry for them, having to live in a dump like this."

"Let's check the back," I said.

We walked down the hallway and the smell grew stronger. I followed the scent past a bathroom before coming to the bedroom. The smell intensified in the bedroom. A large window on the back wall stood open. There wasn't a bed, or any other furniture in the room. Large vines grew in through the open window. They curled around, filling a corner of the room forming a kind of nest. Plenty of water had come in through the window over the years, leaving a mat of leaves and small plants growing on the floor. A bird took flight, rushing out the window. I could feel the floor flexing from our weight.

It may sound like a strange scene, and I suppose it would be for someone unfamiliar with forest trolls. What I found strange was a large black puddle around the nest. I knelt beside it and gave it a whiff. It was definitely the source of the smell. I didn't know how or why it was here.

I stuck the end of my finger in the puddle. It was viscous and sticky. "Got some tar."

"Shit," Holt said. "That's more than some. What the hell did that?"

I shrugged. "Your guess is as good as mine."

"I guess Eddie's gone," Holt said.

I understood why he felt that way. With as many people as we had seen disappear, I was almost getting used to it. None of the missing people had come back, there wasn't a ransom, or any demands. Up until now there weren't any clues.

"Let's not give up just yet," I said. "We're not going to pack up and go home because we found a puddle."

Holt sighed. "I wish we had some dust. We could track them pretty easy if we did."

"Yeah, well . . . if ifs and buts were pixie dust—"

"Take a look at this," he said.

Holt pointed at a mark on the wall. It was a troll's three fingered handprint smeared in tar on the wall beside the closet. The closet door was closed. The floor and walls surrounding the door were black but the door itself remained impossibly clean.

"What the hell?" I muttered.

I picked up a leaf and wiped my finger off on it before joining Holt in front of the closet.

"You don't think there's something in there?"

"Krasis," I said before making the change to my half human, half otter form.

When Holt completed his change I motioned toward the closet with my head.

Holt shook his head. "You open it," he whispered. "I don't want something jumping out to eat my face like last time. It's the diving bell all over again."

"I told you to knock on the bell and I would handle the meat but you didn't want to. If you had done as you were told you would've been fine."

He looked from me to the door and back. "This is different."

I pointed to him and then to the closet and mouthed the words *open it.*

He gave me a scowl before stepping up to the closet. I readied my blade when I felt something cold and wet on my foot. I looked down to see the tar covering my foot. It confused me a little since I shouldn't have stepped in it from where I was standing. It quickly made sense as the tar started to move up my leg.

"Holt," I said trying to pull my foot free.

The tar held onto my foot. I say *held on* because it wasn't just sticky, it had grip. This stuff was alive.

"What do we do?" he shouted.

I pulled my foot up leaving a string of tar and lifted my blade above my head. I hesitated for a second, imagining my blade getting stuck as well. Ultimately it was the only chance I had to get unstuck. I brought the blade down as hard as I could. It cut cleanly through the string. The pull on my leg suddenly released and I fell backward against the wall. The tar fell away onto the floor and moved back to join the larger puddle. I jumped to the right and Holt to the left as the puddle lunged in our direction. I moved back into the hallway as the puddle spread out in the floor. Holt was cut off by the closet.

"Jump over it," I said.

The tar puddle was only a couple feet wide by the wall, he could easily clear it. Holt nodded and leapt over the puddle. He cleared it, at least he would have, if the tar hadn't lurched up from the floor and grabbed his legs. Holt slammed down onto the floor in front of the door. I stuck my blade in the wall and grabbed him by the arm. I tried to pull him out of the tar. It seemed to be pulling him back into the puddle at the same time that it slowly moved up his body.

Holt grabbed the doorframe. "Get this shit off me!"

I took a few swings with my blade. The tar split from where I struck and then filled back in almost immediately. The tar engulfed his lower body and flowed slowly up his torso. I wasn't going to be able to cut it off him without taking pieces of him off with it. I'd have to find another solution.

"Don't let go," I said, turning and running down the hallway towards the kitchen. I needed to find something to stop the tar. How do you fight a liquid? If I could freeze it that would probably work. I picked up a roll of paper towels off the counter and wondered how many rolls it would take to soak up a tar monster.

"Obie!" Holt shouted. "Hurry up. It's—"

His cries for help were replaced with gagging followed by muffled screaming. I could imagine the black sludge covering his face and oozing down his throat. There wasn't another option, a last resort. I grabbed a bottle of vegetable oil and doused it over the paper towel. I turned the knob of the stove hoping there was some gas in the tank outside. The stove clicked a few times and fire jumped up from the eye. I lit my makeshift torch and ran back down the hallway.

Burning it wasn't an ideal option. It would mean a lot of pain for Holt, both now and during the healing process that would follow. There wasn't an alternative at this point. How I felt about it didn't matter, I couldn't let it take him. When I made it back, the room was clean. All traces of tar were gone, and Holt was gone with it.

CHAPTER 6

I stared at the room in disbelief. The tar around the closet was still there, and the handprint, but the rest was gone and Holt with it. The smoke detector's alarm brought me back to reality. I had all but forgotten that I was holding a burning roll of paper towels billowing black smoke. I went to the bathroom and doused the flames in the tub, leaving the charred roll behind. I grabbed a crumpled up towel from the floor and fanned the smoke detector until it went silent. I tossed the towel into the hallway and knelt in the doorway. I found claw marks Holt left in the doorframe and the cuts in the floor from where I had tried to cut the tar away from him. There wasn't any other sign that he had been there at all.

A bird flew in through the window, landing on one of the vines next to the nest. It chirped a couple times, jumped around the nest, and flew away. I walked over to look out the window. The forest was quiet. I could smell the leaves and trees and the faint scent of tar. After the screeching of the smoke detector, it seemed peaceful.

I heard a thump behind me. It sounded like it came from the closet. I moved, my blade ready. *Could Holt have made it into the closet?* I thought. *And if he did, what happened to all the tar?* I turned the door handle. I jumped back as the door swung open. The closet was full of roots and vines.

Forest trolls could manipulate vegetation. They used their magic to form nests like the one in the bedroom and stay hidden. In extreme circumstances, they used it to defend themselves. Trolls get a bad rap in pop culture but the truth is, I've never met a troll I didn't like. They're some of the most kind and gentle people you'll ever run across.

I leaned an arm against the doorframe. "Eddie . . . You in there?"

I didn't get a response, but an intact cocoon told me he was. I went to work with my blade. It took me a couple minutes to make a hole large enough to see inside. Eddie was in there all right. He was unconscious, collapsed on the floor.

"Eddie," I said. "Wake up."

He didn't respond so I went to work clearing the cocoon enough to get him out. After a little work I made the hole large enough to pull him through. It was then I discovered not all the tar had gone. He was covered in it head to toe. I laid him out on the floor. I got the towel from the hallway and wiped what I could off of his face. The tar that was on him didn't seem to be alive. Maybe if it got too far from the central mass it severed its connection with . . . whatever that was.

I sheathed my blade and knelt beside him. "Eddie, you alright?"

He didn't answer. I gave him a couple pats on the cheek. Still nothing. I held a hand over his chest and channeled healing energy into him. It flowed over him almost immediately, telling me he wasn't physically injured.

"Alright, let's go," I said.

I heaved him onto my shoulders in a fireman's carry and headed for the truck. Maybe Doc Lin could figure out what was wrong with him. I made it outside and halfway to the truck when I stopped in my tracks. I patted my pockets looking for my keys. They weren't there. Holt drove over and hadn't given them back to me before he was abducted. I didn't see them in the ignition or on the console. Holt must still have them. I took Eddie back inside and laid him down on the couch, pulled out my phone, and called Doc Lin.

She sounded half asleep and whispered when she answered. "Hello."

"Hey, Doc, I've got an emergency. I have someone here that needs your help, and we could use a ride to the clubhouse."

"Obie, I just got home. I had a late night at the uh . . . hospital." I could hear the agitation in her voice. "I'm not a taxi."

"I never said you were. I would've called Hank but like I said, I got someone here that needs your help, so I had to call you anyway." There was silence on the other end. After twenty seconds I was starting to think we got disconnected. "Doc? You there?"

"Send me the address," she whispered.

I hung up and texted her Eddie's address. Now all I had to do was wait. With nothing to do my thoughts turned to Holt and the tar. I couldn't wrap my head around where they had gone. I did a lap around the house, looked through every room inside and even opened the door to the crawlspace. I came up with nothing. Not a trace of tar on anything but Eddie and the closet. I was starting to understand what happened to all the folks that had gone missing lately. I figured someone or something had been taking them but until now I had no idea of *how* they were doing it.

There was a bright side. Thera should be able to direct me to where Holt was. With her help I could track him down in no time. He might even lead me to the other missing Ultras. I changed back to my human form and sat in the doorway of the trailer to wait for Doc Lin. I looked back to see Eddie was still passed out on the couch. He hadn't moved an inch.

"Thera," I said. "Holt's in trouble. I need your help."

There wasn't a response.

"Thera. I really need to talk to you," I said. "It's important."

Thera made sure all Keepers knew that we worked for her. At the same time, when we called, most of the time she came. If she would help or not was anyone's guess. This seemed to be one of the occasions she decided not to show. I'd get Eddie to the clubhouse and try again. I could always annoy her into showing if I had to. I'd avoid that strategy if I could, she wouldn't be in the best mood if I'd pestered her into paying attention to me. After twenty minutes Doc Lin's Mercedes pulled in behind my truck, Thera still hadn't responded. I went inside, picked up Eddie, and carried him out.

She opened the back door of the car and closed it when she saw us coming. "What's all over him?"

"Tar, I think."

"It's going to get all over the back seat . . . This is a Mercedes."

"He's hurt," I said.

"Hold on," she said.

She took a newspaper she had in the front and layered the pages to protect the seat. I laid Eddie down in the back. The paper stuck to him which helped in keeping the car clean but didn't do much for him personally.

I got in the passenger seat. "I really appreciate the ride. I hope I haven't put you out any."

The way her face crumpled up told me I had in fact. "What's wrong with him?"

I shrugged. "I was hoping you could tell me. He was attacked by something that left him like this. I healed him but he's not waking up."

She scowled. I'd never seen her in a foul mood before. There's a first time for everything, I guess.

"Umm . . . You okay?" I asked.

She sighed. "Yeah, sorry. Things are a little rough at home."

"Sorry to hear."

"How do you maintain a relationship when you have to keep so many secrets?" she asked.

"Was that a rhetorical question?" I asked.

"I'll take an answer if you have one."

"Well . . . I wish I did, but the truth is I don't really know," I said.

"But you've been in at least one serious relationship. I've heard people talk about it. How did you do it?"

"That was different. Naylet's a nymph. She was on the secret side of things so there really wasn't much I had to keep from her," I said.

"What happened to her?" she asked. "Did it not work out?"

I looked out the window. "It's a long story."

We rode in silence for a few minutes before Doc Lin spoke again. "You've never dated a human?"

"Nah, between the secrecy and lifespan difference . . . I just don't see it working out," I said. "Holt, well . . . I don't think I'd call what he does with human women *dating* but he has more experience with it than I do."

"Speaking of lifespan, How long does a Keeper live exactly?" she asked.

"Indefinitely."

"Is that the gift you get for working for Thera?"

"Being immortal doesn't mean we don't die. It just means we don't die naturally. There's no growing old and passing in your sleep. No chance for a peaceful end. I will die one day; I have no doubt of that. And when I do it will be through violence. It's going to be bad. Violent and painful most likely," I said. "That's not a gift."

"Where is Holt anyway? I thought he'd be your first call if you needed a ride."

I sighed. "That's another long story."

Doc Lin smiled. "Sounds like we're both having a rough day."

We pulled into the junkyard that surrounded Morrison Salvage and the clubhouse of the Tortured Occult Motorcycle Club. Driving up the dirt path through the rusted and parted out vehicles, we parked in front of the clubhouse. We took Eddie out of the back of the car. The newspaper had managed to cover him almost completely during the drive.

I hauled him inside. We got some looks from the patrons enjoying drinks and company around the bar. No one really gave us more than a passing glance. I wish I could say hauling a half-dead ultranatural into the clubhouse was unusual for me. It wasn't.

Adan, the wererat emissary from Atlanta, got up from his usual table in the corner and followed us into the back. We took Eddie to one of the bedrooms and laid him down on the bed. His breathing was slow and steady.

"What happened?" Adan asked.

"I'm not sure honestly." I shrugged.

Adan looked at his phone. "The meeting's in twenty minutes, we're supposed to head over to Ground Zero right after. I think the new doctor is over getting the medical facilities set up. Maybe we should take him?"

I had forgotten about the council meeting I was supposed to be attending today. The council was comprised of the rats, elves, Tortured Occult, myself, and a representative of the masses. It wasn't a perfect system but it was better than no system at all.

"If it resembles a real hospital, then it would be better than this," Doc Lin said.

"Alright," Adan said. "I'll give him a call and let him know you'll be bringing him over."

"Actually, can you give us a ride?" I asked. "I don't have my truck."

"Yeah, no problem." Adan said. "You need anything, Doc?"

"We'll do what we can for him," Doc Lin said. "Can you send someone in please."

"Sure, Doc, no problem," he said. "We'll head over after the meeting."

Adan left me alone with Eddie and Doc Lin. She was holding up one of the troll's eyelids and shining a light on and off his eye when Ginsu walked in.

"Well damn," Ginsu said. "Somebody traded out the feathers for newspaper. That's new. He's only half covered though."

"He's hurt," I said. "It's not the time to make fun of him."

"It ain't that, Obie," Ginsu said. "I just hate to see a job half done. I think we got some down pillows around here somewhere if you want to wrap this up real quick. Worse case I can get a box of napkins. Tarred and napkinned . . . Has a nice ring to it."

Doc Lin turned around and looked Ginsu in the eye. "Shut up and get me some towels, soap, and warm water."

"Must be on the rag," Ginsu mumbled as he left the room.

I didn't know if Doc Lin heard him. Sometimes when you have enhanced senses it's easy to forget that everyone doesn't. If she did hear him, she didn't show it. It might just be that she had gotten used to his uncouth ways in the past few months. Doc Lin had officially decided to study ultranatural biology. Whenever someone had an injury they needed help with, they called Doc Lin.

"Well? I asked.

She clicked the light off and put it in her pocket. "I don't know. Once he's cleaned up, I'll have a better idea. It's going to take a while."

Ginsu came back a minute later with what Doc requested. She used the soapy water to wipe the tar off his face and neck.

"Alright," I said. "Let me know if you need me."

"Obie, wait," Doc Lin said. "He's waking up."

Eddie groaned and opened his eyes just a sliver. He raised a hand to his head and started to sit up.

Doc Lin put a hand on his shoulder to stop him. "Take it easy. You've been through a lot."

"Where am I?" he asked.

"You're at the clubhouse," I said. "I found you in the closet at your house. What do you remember?"

His voice was hoarse. "Water."

"Hold tight," I said.

Tico, the wereraccoon, was tending bar today. I went out to the bar and stood at the end. Tico was wiping down a glass at the other end of the bar. He looked over at me. I gave him a nod. He went back to wiping the glass. I waited through a full minute of being ignored before I walked around the bar to where he was standing.

"I need a glass of water."

"Sounds like a personal problem," he said.

I'd like to think he didn't like me because I rarely ordered anything. That meant no tips for him. I found out the truth the last time the club had a run. He was hung up on my ex and he blamed me for what happened to her and the fact that she was gone now.

I reached behind the bar and grabbed a glass and the soda gun. He didn't try to stop me, probably because he knew if it turned into a fight, I'd trounce him. There were a bunch of buttons on it and I didn't know what any of them stood for. I pushed them, shooting random liquids on the counter until I found the one for water and filled up the cup. When the glass was full I headed to the back.

"You really are a first-class asshole, ain't ya?" Tico called after me.

I turned and pushed the door open with my back, raising the glass as if I was giving him a toast and headed back to Eddie. We sat Eddie up and he downed half the water in two gulps.

"How're you feeling?" Doc Lin asked.

Eddie held his arms out from his body. "Sticky."

Doc Lin passed him a bottle of dish soap. "Get a shower and scrub off all the tar you can. I'm sure you'll feel a lot better. We're going to take you over to Ground Zero to get checked out."

"If Doc clears it, come into the council meeting when you're done. I'd like to update everybody on what's going on and we need to hear your story."

Eddie disappeared into the bathroom and the shower came on.

"Is he going to be alright?" I asked.

Doc Lin sat on the edge of the bed. "We'll have to keep an eye on him, but if there's no other issues besides being covered in tar and exhausted, then he should make a full recovery."

CHAPTER 7

I was next to last to walk in the conference room. Hank, the werebear leader of the Tortured Occult Motorcycle Club, looked at the clock. I never got the impression he cared for council meetings, but he was a good sport about them. He understood the importance of working together to maintain order. Adan sat beside him with Queen Isabelle across the table. She'd settled into her responsibilities as Queen well. She was young for a Queen, it's true, still a child really but many of us aren't afforded the luxury of choosing when we grow up. She seemed to have aged a few years, by human standards, in the past few months, making her seem like a mature human child of twelve or thirteen.

I slid the chair up to the table and took a seat.

"You're late," Hank said. "Anyone seen Hambone?"

"I'm here," Hambone said, walking through the door. "Apologies, it couldn't be avoided."

Kobolds resembled half human-half coyotes. Hambone's most distinguishing feature was his weight. Big boned would be a nice way to describe him, morbidly obese would be another. He was carrying a white box with a big birthday cake in it.

"Could you stick this on the table for me please?" He held the box out to me.

I looked through the plastic on the top of the box. It was decorated in white buttercream with blue detailing. It read, Happy Eighty Seven point five Hambone. Eighty-seven was a little over middle age for a kobold. Probably well over for Hambone considering how poorly he took care of himself.

"I didn't know it was your point five already," I said, sliding the box in front of the empty chair. "Happy point five!"

His chest puffed with pride and he flashed me a smile that ran from ear to ear. "Thanks, Obie! I've been looking forward to it for months."

"Probably about six," I said, pulling Hambone's chair away from the table for him.

"Roughly," he said.

We waited patiently, for the most part, as he hoisted himself into his chair. It took him a full minute of effort and three tries but he eventually made it. By the time he pulled it off he was panting and out of breath.

"What's a point five?" Isabelle asked.

Hambone took gasping breaths as he spoke. "Well Queen . . . Isabelle . . . I understand that . . . I may . . . not . . . be as long lived . . ." He held up a finger and took a moment to catch his breath. "Ahem . . . Long lived as a kobold without some of my health concerns. I decided to pack all the joy from those years I expect to lose into what I have left so I doubled the frequency of my birthdays. I celebrate my actual birthday and six months later, today, I have a point five."

"I'm sorry, I didn't know," Isabelle said. "I would have brought you a present. It was nice of you to bring cake for everyone though."

Hambone's coyote-like jaws flapped in shock. "Everyone? Well . . . I mean . . . Obie doesn't eat, especially cake," Hambone said, looking over at me. "It would be rude for everyone to eat in front of him . . . Wouldn't it?"

Isabelle smiled. "I'm just playing. Have a very merry point five."

"You really had me going there." Hambone chuckled. "All right then."

He opened the box with reverence. Drool pooled up on his tongue and dripped onto his considerable girth. He leaned in slowly, inhaling the delicate aromas. He gingerly licked a bit of frosting off a corner of the cake. He swirled it in his mouth, savoring the flavor and moaned in pleasure.

"I feel dirty," Adan said. "Can we start already?"

The door opened and Eddie walked in carrying a glass of water. He was a touch over seven feet tall. His skin looked more like bark, rough and light grey with touches of brown. His hair grew in short, thick, and green like moss. I could still see some black from the tar worked into the crevices in his skin.

"This is a private meeting," Hank said.

Eddie stopped in his tracks looking wide eyed at the group around the table.

"I asked him here," I said getting up from my chair. "Have a seat here, Eddie."

Eddie sat at the table looking generally uncomfortable. I stood behind him to address the council.

"We're all aware of the disappearances that have been happening over the past few months. We haven't had any real leads until today. Eddie was almost abducted. Holt and I got there in time to save him. Unfortunately, it took Holt instead. I wanted the council to hear Eddie's story." I turned to Eddie. "Can you tell us what happened?"

"I don't really know. I was at the house. I heard a noise from outside the bedroom window. It sounded like a deer. I went to get a look at it. Next thing I know I'm covered in this black sludge. It'd come through the window as a big mass and just hit me all of a sudden. I tried to get it off at first but then I realized it was alive. It tried to pull me out the window. I figured if it wanted me outside I should go the other way. I made it to the closet and put up roots to seal the door." He paused to finish the rest of the water in the glass. "The tar would come in through the cracks in the roots and suffocate me. I would wake up and the tar would seep in and suffocate me again. It went on like that until you found me. I don't know how long I was in there or how many times I passed out."

"You were in there about a day," I said.

I looked at Hambone. He hadn't seemed to pay attention at all while Eddie updated the council on the morning's adventure. He had made it though about a quarter of the birthday cake. The buttercream frosting and cake crumbs had gotten all over his hands, face, and chest. It was embedded in his fur and fell in clumps on the table.

"Thanks, Eddie," Isabelle said. "We need to talk about it privately, if you don't mind."

Eddie nodded, and left.

As soon as the door closed behind him, Adan said, "What the hell could do something like that?"

"I've never seen anything like it," I said. "There was a puddle of tar in the middle of the bedroom when Holt and I walked in. Like Eddie said, it was alive. We didn't realize it at first but before we knew what was happening it was on us. I figured I'd burn it off of him and went to get some fire. By the time I got back Holt was gone. The thing is, whatever it was moved fast. Once it got Holt it was just gone. It makes sense why we haven't been finding evidence left behind of the people that were taken."

Isabelle turned in her chair to look at Hob. "Do you have any idea what this creature could be?"

"*Nein,* my Queen. I will need more information to make the determination."

"Here's what I want to know." Adan leaned forward and rested an elbow on the table. "You said when this thing disappeared it took all the tar with it, right?"

"Yeah," I said.

"So why is Eddie still covered in the stuff?"

"Huh," I said, shifting back in my chair and looking at the door Eddie had just walked out of. "Maybe it was cut off. Eddie said he was closing himself in with the vines. What if the tar was left behind because he sealed it in with him?"

"It makes sense," Isabelle said. "Do you have a plan to find Holt?"

"Thera should be able to lead me to him but she's not answering me."

Hank sighed heavily and spoke for the first time. "I have been waiting to bring it up, but my son, Torch, is still missing. No one's heard from him for months. He was the first one that disappeared. Isabelle confirmed that the Queen, the old Queen, didn't get him." He paused and shook his head. "I know you've all been looking for him and I appreciate it. I need to find my son."

"Does anyone have any dust?" asked Adan. "We could do a tracking spell."

Everyone looked at each other around the table. After a few seconds it was clear no one was coming forward about a dust stash they had squirreled away. I wasn't going to mention I'd had some earlier.

"There's just not a lotta dust to go around right now," I said. "First Torch and now Holt. This is officially getting out of control. The good news is, when I can get Thera to answer me she can lead us to them, assuming it was the same thing that took them both."

"You think something else happened to Torch?" Isabelle asked.

I shrugged. "It's too soon to tell. I mean, it's our best lead."

Hambone spit masticated cake all over the table when he spoke. "It's a big problem! The longer we go without dust the more trouble it's going to be. It's going to be pandemonium! Murder in the streets! We have to do something, and we have to do it quick."

"I know you don't want to hear it but there's nothing we can do about it right now," Adan said. "The new facility will be completed as soon as possible."

"And after it's finished how long before it's up and running?" Hambone asked.

Adan ran a hand over his rat snout. "We still have to move the equipment in. Some of it's going to have to be made special. Willix estimates another couple months to get everything up and running before we can start dusting."

Hambone closed the lid of the cake box and sat. He had icing all over his face and his hands. I'd never seen him so upset that he stopped eating.

"And another three months to actually process some dust," Hambone said. "People are disappearing. There are rumors of hunters. We need to get this under control now."

Hank nodded but didn't say anything. He was used to keeping his emotions close to his chest, but I knew it was weighing heavy on his mind. The fact that we were at least five months out from having some dust didn't help.

"Hob, do we have to have all the equipment in place before we start dusting?" Isabelle asked.

Hob stepped up to the table. "*Nein,* the process has many stages. Some of these processes take weeks to complete. It is possible to have the equipment put in place as its needed."

"That'll shave some time off," I said. "We have bodies piling up in the Copper Mines ready to go."

"What about the people that are disappearing?" Hambone shouted, standing up in his chair and slamming his hands on the table. Buttercream icing splattered my shirt.

Hank sat up straight. "Look, no one wants to find out what's going on more than I do but we can only work with what we have. Without dust or a lead there's nothing we can do right now."

"I'll see if our network can round up some dust," Adan said. "If they can, it won't be cheap."

Hambone wiped a hand across his forehead smearing icing into his fur. "Do we know where that dust will come from? We could be buying the people we're trying to save."

"I'm not worried about the cost," Hank said. "And no matter who the dust was made from, if it prevents more folks going missing, it's worth it."

I looked Hank in the eye. "I'll keep trying to contact Thera. She has to respond eventually. We'll find them."

I didn't know if I was trying to reassure myself or him more. The truth was, Thera didn't have to do anything she didn't want to. She could go months without responding to a call; it wouldn't be the first time.

There was a knock at the door.

Hank called, "Yeah, it's open."

Big Ticket stuck his head in. "Sorry to interrupt but we got a problem."

CHAPTER · 8

"About halfway back, behind the grey Crown Vic," Big Ticket said.

Hank stepped up to the window and spread the blinds with a couple fingers. "Hmm," he grunted as he peeked through the hole he made. "Who is it?"

"No idea," B.T. said. "I haven't seen him before."

"What's he doing?" I asked.

The bedroom's second-story window gave us a good vantage point for the west side of the junkyard. It wasn't uncommon for random folks to drive up to the junkyard and look around for a car that might have a part they needed. I wasn't sure why a single person in the junkyard would raise such suspicion.

After a few seconds Hank stepped back from the window. "Just watching."

I peeked through the window. I scanned the junkyard, my eyes going from car to car looking for the grey car Big Ticket said this mystery man was hiding behind. I felt as if I was playing a game of Where's Waldo, junkyard edition. I was beginning to think I would have to ask one of them to point him out when I saw a glint of light from behind a lime green Volkswagen Beetle. Someone was peeking up just behind the hood with a pair of binoculars. The window hadn't been cleaned in maybe ever and had a hazy film that prevented me from discerning much.

Hank sighed. "Do you know how long he's been there?"

Big Ticket shook his head. "I got you as soon as we found him. I told everybody to stay out of sight."

"Get everybody ready, human form with weapons," Hank said, walking toward the door. "I'll go see what he's doing."

I followed him. "I'm curious about this one. I'll come with you, okay?"

"Suit yourself."

I followed Hank down the stairs and out the back door of the clubhouse, opting for a stealthy approach. If he was going to act like he was up to no good, the least we could do was play along. We cut across the junkyard of Morrison Salvage, staying low to avoid being seen. We weaved our way through the cars to the fence and then turned west, following it around behind the intruder.

We worked our way quietly, being careful not to disclose our presence. We moved up a few cars behind the intruder. It was a man wearing brown penny loafers complete with pennies in them, khakis, and a navy polo. Whoever this guy was, he was dressed too nicely to be creeping around in a junkyard. I didn't get the impression we had to work so hard to sneak up on him. He was focused on the clubhouse, still looking though the binoculars.

"What do you think?" Hank whispered. "Should we jump him?"

I shrugged. "Let's see what he's doing here first."

Hank held up two fingers, motioning to move forward. We went around opposite sides of the car we were crouching behind. We positioned ourselves behind the intruder about five feet apart. When we were in position I gave Hank a nod.

"You must be lost?" Hank said.

The man spun around, dropping the binoculars. He was Asian, Japanese maybe. What concerned me more than his motivation was the revolver tucked into his pants.

"If you need a part you can talk to one of the mechanics at the shop," Hank said. "If not, you need to go."

He grabbed the piece, pointing it at me, then Hank, then back to me. "I'm not leaving until I get what I came for."

We were far enough apart that he couldn't cover both of us at the same time. His hands shook enough to give the gun's barrel a noticeable quiver. Sweat dotted his forehead and soaked into his shirt. His eyes were wide and strained, the eyes of a desperate man. He definitely wasn't a professional, this was personal for him. He looked like a guy in over his head and he knew it. That made him unpredictable, and unpredictable people were dangerous.

"You got some real stones, I'll give you that," Hank said, more amused than threatened. "Do you have any idea of the shit storm that's about to rain down on you?"

His eyes darted back and forth. "Shut up, I have the gun so I'm in charge." He jerked the gun in Hank's direction and pulled the hammer back. "No one's going to do anything as long as I have a gun on you."

"What do you want?" I asked.

He whipped the gun to point it at me. "You, I know you have Rebecca Lin inside. You're going to stay here with me and he's going to go bring her out. If you try anything funny your friend here's going to get it."

Hank smirked. "You think he practiced that line in the mirror?"

"He sounds like he's in a bad detective novel," I said.

He shouted, "Shut the hell up! I'm not going to tell you again."

I held my hands chest high. I wanted him to think I was surrendering. I took a step forward. "Hey buddy, I'm not sure what you think's going on—"

The gun went off. The man flinched from the sound as a percussive wave hit me. The bullet whizzed to my right shattering the window of the car behind me. I looked at Hank. He was running out of patience. The clubhouse was well outside the city and a single shot wasn't necessarily something that would draw a lot of attention. If he kept shooting and someone a little nosy happened to drive by and saw it, we would have a much bigger mess on our hands. Police weren't welcome or wanted at the clubhouse.

"Hurry up if you're going to do something," Hank said.

The man thought he was speaking to him. "I didn't mean to do that. I don't want to hurt anybody."

Being faster and stronger than the average bear often comes in handy. I rushed forward and grabbed the man's gun hand. Bending his wrist, I pointed the gun harmlessly to the side and delivered a right cross to his face. His head whipped from the impact. He let go of the gun and his body went limp and he fell face first in the dirt. He lay still.

I held the gun. Opening the cylinder of the revolver I found five bullets. I pulled one out and looked at it. Just a simple hollow point, not silver. It was the last bit of evidence to confirm my suspicion; he had no idea who he was messing with.

I tossed the gun to Hank. "Do you recognize him?"

"Nope," Hank said. "Let's get him inside quick."

Hank picked him up and heaved him over one shoulder. The road was visible from where we were standing but it was still early. Only one car passed in the time it took to us to carry him to the clubhouse. He was still unconscious when we took him inside. Doc Lin was sitting at the bar. Her face went pale when she saw Hank and the man over his shoulder.

She stood. "Hank, hold on a second," she said. "I know him."

Hank ignored Doc Lin but when he spotted Cotton he said, "We need a deadbolt put on the back bedroom."

I pulled Doc Lin aside as Hank disappeared into the back. "Who is he?"

She sighed. "My husband. What did you do to him?"

"He was sneaking around in the junkyard and pulled a gun on me and Hank," I said. "I defended myself."

"Did you kill him?"

I put a hand to my chest and feigned shock. "Rebecca! Don't you know me better than that?"

"Obie . . ."

I shrugged. "I punched him in the face. What'd ya want?"

"I want you to not beat up my husband."

"I want to not get shot at," I said.

Hank returned and joined us.

"It's Doc's husband," I said.

"What the hell's he doing here?" Hank asked.

Doc Lin looked mortified. "Well, I haven't been home much lately, the work I'm doing over here is taking up a lot of time, not to mention being on call all hours. He's been getting suspicious. I told him I've been working overtime at the hospital. He must have followed me here."

"He's staying until we figure out what to do with him," Hank said.

"What do you mean *what to do with him?*" Doc Lin asked, panic creeping into her voice.

We all knew what it meant. Besides the normal issue of risking the secrecy of our world, he had come to the club house with a gun. That alone was enough to at least get him a beating by the club.

Hank looked her in the eye before he turned to me. "You need a ride to Ground Zero?"

"Adan's got us," I said.

He walked away. "I'll see you over there."

When he had disappeared through the door Doc Lin turned to me. "Obie, you've got to help me."

"Hank's pissed and rightly so. He brought a gun with him," I said. "This is really club business so there may not be much I can do."

"They listen to you," Doc Lin said. "If you vouch for him they'll have to let him go."

"Vouching for someone I don't know and took a shot at me might be a problem," I said. "I'll try to help, but believe me, they don't *have* to do anything. Let's go check him out and then we have to get Eddie over to Ground Zero."

Doc got a rag and some water. We went to the bedroom Hank had put him in. Cotton stood guard in front of the door.

"Is he awake?" I asked.

Cotton shrugged. "Hell if I know."

We went in. He was sprawled on the bed, still unconscious.

Doc Lin rushed to the bed. "Will . . .? Can you hear me?"

She repositioned him with his head on the pillow. He had a pretty serious bloody nose and his eyes had already turned black. I'd got him a little better than I'd realized. The blood had gotten smeared around his face in transport. He looked like hell.

Doc Lin turned back to me. "Obie, heal him."

I put a hand over his head channeling healing energy into him. He started to wake. I moved back to stand by the door.

Doc Lin sat over him on the bed. "Will? Can you hear me?"

Will opened his eyes. "Rebecca?"

She put a hand on the side of his face. "Are you okay?"

He sat up, touching a couple fingers to his nose. They came away bloody. He wiped the blood onto his pants. "My car's parked down the street," he whispered. "I packed a few essentials and have a couple plane tickets to Vancouver. We just have to get to the car."

Doc Lin didn't whisper when she replied. "Do you think I'm a hostage or something?"

"You're not?" Will asked. "Then what are you doing here?"

"I'm working."

"Working . . ." Will took the rag from her and cleaned blood on his own. "I called the hospital. They said you hadn't worked there in a couple months. You're telling me you left your job as Chief of Medicine to work in a biker bar?"

"It's complicated." She sighed. "You've caused a lot of problems by coming here."

"You've been distant, secretive . . . At first I thought you were having an affair. Now I don't know what's going on but I'm the one that's causing problems? It's time for you to tell me the truth."

Doc Lin looked over at me. I shook my head as subtly as possible.

"What are you looking at him for?" He asked.

"I told you I was working and that is true," she said.

"You told me you were working at the hospital," he said.

Doc Lin sighed. "I know, I'm sorry."

There was a knock at the door. I opened it a crack.

Adan was standing on the other side in krasis. "We need to hit the road. We're already gonna be late."

"We're coming," I said.

"So you're going then?" Will asked.

"We can talk more when I get back."

I opened the door a little more and Doc Lin slid out of the room. I was about to follow when Will stopped me.

"Hey." He paused to spit some blood out on the floor. "Nice right."

I gave him a nod and followed Doc Lin outside to Adan's car. Eddie and Adan were leaning against the truck, waiting for us.

When he saw us, Eddie came over. "Hey, Doc, look I'm just a little tired. I'm not hurt. What do you say we call off this whole checkup thing and I'll just get some rest?"

Doc Lin let out a heavy sigh. "Nothing would make me happier than to blow it off, but we need to get you checked out, just to be sure. We don't want any surprises, okay?"

Eddie nodded. "Alright."

CHAPTER • 9

"Shotgun," Hambone said.

Eddie had just got into the back seat of Adan's car. I was standing with the passenger door open, about to claim my seat. Hambone was still covered in frosting and cake crumbs. Pretending I didn't hear him, I jumped in the seat. He would probably complain about it the entire ride but he was always going on about something.

When Adan saw Hambone, he said, "Hold up, you're not getting in the car like that."

"What?" Hambone was genuinely confused as to the problem. "I left the rest of the cake. What's the matter?"

"You're going to get icing everywhere."

Hambone shrugged. "Well, I don't have another ride so . . ."

"Go clean up. We'll wait," Adan said.

"Fine," Hambone said.

He sulked over to the spigot on the side of the clubhouse, complaining the entire way. After a couple minutes of scrubbing in cold water he looked eighty-five percent cleaner and one hundred percent miserable.

He climbed into the seat behind me, looking generally sour. "I don't see what all the fuss is about. It was just a few crumbs and a touch of frosting."

Adan started the car and drove down to the road. As we pulled onto the pavement I heard faint crunching coming from the back seat. Adan turned around to look at Hambone.

"Are you eating?" Adan asked.

Hambone held up his hands to show they were empty but kept his mouth shut. Adan turned back around. I watched Hambone in the side mirror. He sat still for a few seconds and then his jaw moved slowly down and back up. The same subtle crunch emerged from the back seat again. Adan sighed as Hambone discreetly munched. Queen Isabelle's motorcade, her SUV and two guard trucks, and Hank on his Harley, pulled out behind us.

With the old dusting facility destroyed and Hob working with Queen Isabelle, we had to find a new location and someone to run it. Willix was a no brainer to run the facility. He had been working with Hob ever since he lost the council election to Hambone in '84. He seemed happy to have the opportunity to continue his work. That was the easy part. Construction of a new facility with the required equipment was the bigger issue. For that we turned to the wererats. The rats had mini cities for ultranaturals called undergrounds set up in almost every major city across the world. You could find an underground from Atlanta to Beijing to Hamburg and everywhere in between. The T.O. was resistant at first to allow the rats a foothold so deep in their territory but in the end they relented.

We drove into Dawson Forest ten minutes away. It was an undeveloped area of land in North Georgia officially owned by the city of Atlanta. Unofficially, it belonged to the wererats. It had been a nuclear test site in the sixties. There were still a few concrete structures scattered around the property. We called the largest of them Ground Zero.

Adan made a couple turns on the dirt roads running through the forest and then veered off the road driving down a hillside to a creek at the bottom. Instead of crossing the creek he turned and drove downstream.

I expected a rough ride from the rocks that inevitably lined the bottom. To my surprise, it was smooth. We followed the creek around a hundred yards through a slight turn to a giant concrete culvert disappearing into the hillside. It looked like a drainpipe. A small steady stream of water ran out from the bottom. Adan drove into the pipe.

"Where's the water coming from?" I asked.

"While we were excavating the area we hit a spring. We're using it as a water source. The excess is diverted out the pipe and to the creek," Adan said.

"Is the site off grid then?"

"It'll be completely self sufficient and concealed. Many streams and one large river flow through the forest. We've set up hydropower generators to provide all the electricity the facility will need," Adan said. "When it's all done, someone could stand by the front door and never know we're here."

The culvert dead-ended into a concrete wall. Water flowed from a smaller pipe coming out of the side wall. Adan pulled up a small ramp and stopped in front of the wall. There was a loud *ka-chunk,* and the wall swung open. Adan drove forward into a parking deck that looked like it belonged in an airport or train station. The parking deck was empty except for a few work trucks parked in the far corner. It looked new with pristine yellow lines painted on the pavement. Lights hung from the ceiling with arrows directing the flow of traffic. Adan pulled forward, ignoring the arrows, to a spot up front with Queen Isabelle and Hank close behind. We got out and congregated around the vehicles. Isabelle, Yarwor, and the guards from two trucks joined us.

"Yarwor will escort me. The rest of you stay with the vehicles please," Isabelle instructed as Doc Lin and Eddie climbed out of the car.

When Adan had our attention, he began, "Welcome to the new Ground Zero. This is the parking deck, we have sixty spaces. The first floor is complete and we're about seventy percent through the second floor. If you'll follow me . . ."

Adan led us to a security booth built into the back wall. It had a door on either side. The door on the left looked plain, except it had two doorknobs. One in the normal position and one about a foot lower. The door on the right only had one doorknob but it had a red cross in a circle designating it as a hospital entrance. A wererat sat at a console in the booth, sipping a cup of coffee and monitoring multiple screens. He was dressed in a plain gray uniform with UPD embroidered above the left chest pocket.

"This is our first point of security. This booth monitors all incoming and outgoing traffic. The booth is always manned by at least one member of the Underground Police Department." Adan pointed as he spoke as if he was a flight attendant. "There are multiple entrances around Dawson Forest that converge into the east and west tunnels." Adan pointed to hallways on either side of the parking deck. "All of those entrances are hidden and locked. This booth monitors them. There is a separate booth for internal security which I will show you in a moment. The door to your right is the emergency entrance to the hospital. The door to your left leads into Ground Zero. Doc, you want to take Eddie through there and we'll catch up to you."

"Sure," Doc Lin said.

She walked with Eddie to the hospital door. The guard pushed a button, a buzzer sounded and the door released, opening a crack.

Adan asked, "Does anyone have any questions before we continue?"

"Tell me about the Underground Police," Hank said. "What's going on there?"

"The wererats have a single government with uniform laws. You can walk in Underground London to Underground Tokyo and the laws are the same. The UPD enforces those laws."

"Think of the bureaucracy," Hambone said. His eyes glazed over as if he were dreaming of cheesecake. "Red tape for miles!"

"What happens if they arrest you?" Hank asked. "Is the Tortured Occult expected to be held accountable to these laws."

"This is a wererat facility. Anyone that sets foot inside will be expected to conduct themselves in accordance with rat law. This facility isn't completed so things are a little more lax for our tour. For example, most weapons are prohibited inside the Collective Underground. Today though we won't worry about it. Which takes us to our next part of the tour. If you'll follow me please."

We walked through the two-handled door leading into Ground Zero. The bottom handle opened the bottom half of the door for people closer to Hambone's size and the top door handle opened the full door. We entered into a hallway with a door on the end and a row of lockers built into the right wall. The left wall was a second security desk, much larger than the previous one. The glass spanned the entire hallway with multiple officers manning multiple counters.

"All cities in the Collective Underground have a place to keep prohibited items during your stay," Adan said. "You're free to carry your weapons today but after Ground Zero is officially open you will need to either get a permit or stow them in these lockers. This is the main security office. If you are interested in applying for a weapons permit you can do that here. In fact, we'll go ahead and get you what you need." Adan turned to the officer manning the counter and said, "Can we get five welcome pamphlets and weapon permit applications please?"

The officer retrieved some papers from a filing cabinet. He placed them in an electric drawer like you would see in a bank drive through and hit the button to slide the drawer out to us. Adan passed out papers.

I looked at the pamphlet. WELCOME TO THE UNDERGROUND! HERE'S WHAT YOU NEED TO KNOW.

Adan moved to the door on the far side of the room. A sign affixed to the door read YOU ARE NOW ENTERING GROUND ZERO. We stepped through into an upscale looking shopping plaza. It had generous lighting which almost made it feel like we were outside. The center of the plaza was planted with bushes and grass. Pillars ran down either side, floor to ceiling. Shops were built into the walls.

"We have space for twenty-two businesses, not including the hospital and bank. We're still reviewing vendor applications. You can expect restaurants and night life, as well as clothing and grocery stores that cater to the wants and needs specific to the ultranatural community."

Tables with red-and-white checkered tablecloths were outside one of the stores. "What's that place?" I asked.

We followed Adan down the left side of the plaza. "Whisker's Café. It's pretty good. They aren't officially open, of course, but they have been serving the workers and staff getting Ground Zero ready. You're all welcome to stop for a bite when we're finished. At the end of the plaza will be the Department of Records which I'm sure you'll all be using from time to time."

"What's the Department of Records?" Hambone asked.

"The DoR handles driver's licenses, birth certificates, deeds, permits . . . Any documentation necessary for the human world can be acquired for a nominal fee and a short wait," Adan said. "If you'll follow me downstairs, I'll show you the part of the complex most people don't get to see."

CHAPTER 10

Adan led us to a door beside the Department of Records. He pulled a keycard from his pocket and swiped it on a black pad mounted beside the door. Locks released with an audible *click.* He opened the door and held it for us. We walked down a flight of concrete stairs and exited through another door into a hallway. This was much plainer than the plaza. It was just gray concrete walls and floors without any decoration. Doors with keypads lined the hallway. I could hear construction noise from multiple directions.

Adan moved ahead of me. "These rooms will be used for the management of the facility. They house the machinery needed to run the facility. They are finishing construction on office space right now. Nothing we need to get into. The dusting facility is this way."

We followed Adan through a door at the end of the hall. We stepped into a large empty room. It had tile floors with drains and an industrial sink on the wall beside us. It looked like a laboratory without any equipment. Three doors lined the far wall. Adan opened one of the doors revealing a walk-in freezer. It was reminiscent of a meat packing plant, but instead of hunks of beef, an assortment of demon carcasses were suspended by hooks.

"It was built to the specifications Hob provided. Willix has been overseeing the construction, but I'm not sure if he's here now," Adan said. "This is the space for dust production and storage. Not much to see at the moment. We've already moved the corpses that were being stored in the copper mines. Going forward you should bring all bodies here."

I stepped into the freezer for a closer look at the frozen-solid carcasses. The copper mines were chilly but weren't cold enough to keep them from rotting, however slowly. Their time in the mines hadn't been kind to them. The oldest of them had decomposed quite a bit. It didn't instill a lot of confidence in me that we were going to get the dust we needed in three months. The degradation had to have an effect on the quality, quantity, or both.

"Let me show you where you'll drop off the fresh ones," Adan said.

He opened a door that lead to another parking deck. This one was much smaller than the first. There looked to be only one way in, a cargo elevator on the far side of the room. There were clearly marked arrows leading from the elevator, around the parking deck, and back to the other side of the elevator. An automatic carwash was on the right side of the parking deck.

"When you bring a body for dusting you will drive onto the service elevator. Pull up in front of this door," Adan said motioning toward the freezer. "The bodies will be unloaded and weighed. After that, if your truck is dirty you can clean it up quick with our automated carwash. You don't have to spray your truck down with a garden hose anymore. There are also restrooms with showers behind the carwash where you can get cleaned up, if needed. Once you're ready, drive back on the elevator and be on your way.

"Seems simple enough," I said.

"If you'll accompany me onto the elevator we'll get you back to your vehicles," Adan said.

Adan pulled up a gate and we stepped onto the elevator. It was a large industrial style model with plenty of room to move around in, even if there was a truck inside. Adan pulled the gate closed. He hit the button marked ONE and it brought us back up to the parking deck where we started. "Does anyone have any questions?"

"What would you recommend at the Whisker's Café?" Hambone asked.

Adan smiled. "Ask for the stout pie."

"Stout . . . pie . . . It really was a lovely tour," Hambone said, backing away from us. "Isabelle, Obie, etcetera, it's always good—" He jogged toward the café without finishing his sentence.

The rest of the group started walking toward their vehicles. It occurred to me Hank had been unusually quiet. The Tortured Occult had been through a lot of changes in the past six months. The change in leadership after Otis was killed would be enough to cause some serious turmoil. Along with a new identity came a new kutte. The old kutte had a bear's head made of oak leaves, now it was just a bear skull with a pentacle surrounding it. It was a much more aggressive design. The change in leadership was only part of the trouble the T.O. had been through. The trouble with Chisel had caused some internal strife and Torch's disappearance hadn't helped either.

I caught up to Hank. "You hardly said anything the whole time. You doing okay?"

"I've got my mind on other things," he said.

"Torch?"

Hank nodded.

I tried to sound reassuring. "I'll get Thera to lead me to Holt and the people that took Torch. I'm sure we're going to find your boy."

Hank stopped and looked me in the eyes. "If they have him there's no way he's still alive. They've had him over four months already."

"We'll find him. We won't stop until we do," I said.

"Thanks, Obie, I appreciate it." He didn't sound reassured. "I sent a prospect for your keys. He should be here soon. He'll give you a ride to your truck."

Movement out of the corner of my eye caught my attention. Adan was waving for me.

"Thanks, Hank. I'll let you know what I find out."

I went to see what Adan wanted. He held out a card. It was a black card with a red stripe down the middle. It read PINES across the top and Chestatee Reginal Library System in white lettering. There was a barcode with a letter and number combination on the bottom of the card.

"A library card?" I asked. "It doesn't look right."

"That's because it's not a library card," Adan said. "It's your Underground Passport. You use it for everything you need in any Underground worldwide. It will open doors at your access level or below. It's linked to your bank account so you can use it to pay at all the shops or take cash out of the ATM. I took care of your weapons permit as well. If the UPD hassles you about your blade, just give them this card. Oh, and if you *did* want to go to the library it works there too."

I became aware of a rumbling sound coming from the direction of the entrance to the parking deck. As it grew louder, I recognized it as a motorcycle of the hog variety. Something the T.O. would be proud to deafen random strangers with. The rumble dropped to an idle and the concrete door slid open. The engine thumped to life and the biker rode slowly in. I didn't recognize him; he must be new. He looked over at Hank who pointed in our direction.

He pulled up beside us. "You Obie?"

I nodded. "Have something for me?"

He reached into the pocket on his kutte and produced the spare keys to my truck. "I'll take you to your truck when you're ready."

"I'm ready now." I slid the card and keys into my pocket and got on the back of the bike. "Thanks, Adan."

"Good luck finding Holt," Adan said.

"What's your name?" I asked when we pulled up to the exit.

"Officially, prospect," he said, throwing a thumb to the kutte he was wearing.

"How about unofficially?"

The door swung open and he drove down the tunnel.

"Jim," he said. "Hey, next time maybe let the folks at your house know someone's coming over, it almost got ugly."

"Who's at my house?" I asked.

"Some cougar and . . . well, hell, I don't know what he was. Looked like a hairless dog covered in burn scars with an anxiety disorder."

CHAPTER 11

I spent the ride home wondering who Prospect Jim had seen in my house. Could it be possible that Holt escaped the tar? If he managed to set it on fire it would explain the description of a "scarred up dog." Holt wasn't the anxious type though, but I suppose being lit on fire would put anyone on edge.

I had Jim drop me at the end of the driveway. I wanted to know who I was dealing with before they knew I was there. I didn't think they were hostile. If they were waiting to ambush me then they would have killed Jim rather than lose the element of surprise. Then again, if I didn't have keys to get home they'd be waiting around a long time. Maybe they were planning a more up-front attack rather than an ambush . . . or maybe I was just being paranoid. It wouldn't be the first time.

I gave Jim a wave as he drove away. The ultras in my house had no doubt heard the motorcycle. I wanted to wait a few minutes before I went inside. I could walk up through the woods and get an idea who had made themselves at home before they knew I was there. While I waited for the noise from the hog to die off, I decided to give Thera another try.

I closed my eyes and concentrated on Thera. I didn't know how she experienced it when we called her or if the focus would make the "signal" stronger but it was worth a shot.

"I really need to talk to you. Things have gone to shit here and I need some help."

I waited with my eyes closed hoping to hear her ill-tempered voice. I opened one eye and looked around. Nothing. I sighed and opened the mailbox. I had some bills, some junk mail, and a postcard.

The postcard had a picture of buildings I didn't recognize with NEW ORLEANS LOUISIANA plastered across the front. It had a matching postmark on the back with a hand written note.

Heading to Poverty Point and then on to Dallas. Thinking of you and wishing you were here.—N

"Me too." I sighed and put the postcard in my pocket.

The bills and junk mail went back in the mailbox. I walked up the driveway, then around the last turn before the house came into view, and slipped into the woods. I used the trees for cover until I had a good view of the front of the house. An orange Subaru I didn't recognize was parked out front. Lights were on in the house. Whoever was in there wasn't hiding. I watched for a while, catching bits of movement through the living room window.

Waiting wasn't getting me anywhere. Whoever it was had been there for hours already. I could wait for them to come out, but there's no telling how long that would take. I needed to find Holt, this was just getting in the way. No more beating around the bush. I changed to krasis, drew my blade, and walked to the front door.

No sooner had I set foot inside than a woman's voice I recognized called my name from the direction of the living room. "Obie? Is that you?"

I walked toward the living room and ran into Mila. She was a Keeper who worked around Tennessee. She was bound to the mountain lion but when we met in the hallway she was in her human form. She had blond hair buzzed short around the sides and longer and spiked on the top. She wore faded jeans and a red tank top. She was all muscle and curves. She gave me a hug. Her body felt hard and soft at the same time, like steel wrapped in cotton.

"What are you doing here?" I asked.

She pulled away, putting her hands on my cheeks. She squished my face a little and looked deep into my eyes. Her eyes were a light brown, almost matching her hair. "I heard about Naylet . . . Are you okay?"

"Oh yeah," I said, my words distorted the same amount as my mouth. "I'm fine."

She gave me a sad smile. "Obie . . . It's me. Come on."

I put my blade back in its sheath and took her hands. I held them against my chest. "I'm fine, I promise. Even if I wasn't, I have more important things going on. I hear you brought someone with you. I'm guessing this isn't a social visit?"

"Afraid not. This werewolf named Atticus found me and said he had a message for you. It's better if you hear it from him." She turned to the living room but stopped in her tracks. "Oh, and whatever you do don't agitate him. He's been through a lot."

I followed her into the living room. I found a shifter sitting on the mantle of the fireplace. He had a blanket draped around his body with only his muzzle sticking out as if he were doing an impression of Darth Sidious. I couldn't see his eyes, but the blanket shifted slightly, indicating he was looking at me. Mila and I sat on the couch across from him. A couple of fire extinguishers were on the floor in front of the couch. I waited for him to speak but he just sat there breathing deeply.

"I hear you have a message for me?" I said.

"Yes," Atticus said. "You're going to have to bear with me. This is a difficult subject and I have to stay calm. Bad things happen when I get too excited."

"What, you Hulk out or something?"

Mila leaned in and whispered, "He catches on fire."

"What do you mean?"

"He bursts into flames, with all the flailing and screaming you would expect of someone burning alive. If he doesn't keep it together, he'll probably burn your house down."

"Thanks for bringing him inside," I whispered before picking up a fire extinguisher. "Take your time, Atticus, no pressure."

"I had a job with a cable company. I was out on a service call and everything seemed routine. Next thing I know, I'm getting electrocuted. I think it was a trap. Somebody put current where it shouldn't have been. I was taken to a kind of prison. They did some kind of surgery on me and kept me in a special cell where there was water coming out of sprinklers constantly. I was always wet and cold and miserable. I know now it was to keep me from igniting." Atticus paused to take a few deep breaths. "They have a lot of ultras there. They're constantly taking old ones away and bringing new ones in. One day they brought in someone new, a biker by the name of Torch. Long story short, we escaped. I didn't think it was possible, but we actually made it outside. When the shooting started, I burst into flame for the first time. I ran into the river to put myself out. I passed out when I hit the water and woke up washed up against the bank downstream. I don't know what happened to Torch or the other prisoners, but he told me to find a guy named Obie, that he would help me. When I made it back, I asked around and found Mila and here we are."

"Do you know where the prison is?" I asked. "Can you find it again?"

"I don't know the exact location, but we should be able to find it. But if I help you, I want something in return," Atticus said.

"What's that?

"I want you to take me back."

"You want us to return you to the people that took you?" Mila asked.

Atticus took a deep breath. "My cell was the only place where I don't have to worry about catching fire. By all means, get rid of those bastards, but once you do, I'm going back in that cell until somebody can find a way to fix me."

"You got a deal," I said. "Let me just talk to Mila for a minute."

I took Mila outside on the front porch. "Do you trust this guy?"

Mila nodded. "He's at least telling the truth about the fire. I've seen him do it and it's not pretty. There have been people disappearing from my territory for the past few months and this is the first real lead I've had."

"It's been the same here," I said. "I'm not sure exactly how many, more than ten disappeared without a trace . . . Today it was Holt."

Mila looked shocked by the revelation. "Holt was taken?"

"Yeah." I nodded. "It was some kind of living tar. If Atticus can lead us to the abductors, then we might be able to get them back before anything bad happens to them."

"If they took a Keeper we don't need Atticus, Thera can lead us to him. It's bad for Holt but if he can hold out until we can get there then it's the break we need to find them quick."

"You would think so but Thera isn't answering my call. I've tried twice already."

Mila almost shouted when she spoke. "Thera." After a few seconds of no reply she tried again. "We need to speak to you now. We need your help. You need to answer us."

It was a more direct approach than Thera would appreciate. Mila might have taken that tone out of frustration or she could be using a strategy that hadn't occurred to me: Piss Thera off. It was risky but if it got her to reply . . .

Mila threw her hands up in frustration. "How can she not answer? If one of us is in trouble she should show up and help."

"You don't gotta tell me," I said. "We can't make her do anything, so until she decides to talk to us, it is what it is. Atticus is our best bet right now."

"Let's get on the road then," Mila said. "We don't have time to waste."

"You're driving. I don't like the idea of my truck getting blown up."

Mila shot me a smile. "Fair enough."

We got Atticus loaded in the back seat and headed northwest.

"Tell me everything you know about the place," I said.

"Like I said, it's on a river. I saw two bridges when I was brought in. An old one and a new one right beside each other. The old bridge is really old, made of stone. The house is big, three . . . maybe four stories. It was hard to tell. I only got a glimpse of the lights through the woods before the shooting started."

"Anything else?"

Atticus thought for a moment. "I can't be sure, but I think there's a waterfall close by. I heard rushing water, a lot of it. More than just a river."

I pulled up a map on my phone and did a search for bridges in north Georgia. I got a lot of results for covered bridges and not much else.

"Were either of the bridges covered?" I asked.

"No, just normal," Atticus said.

I searched for waterfalls. I scrolled through the results. Ruby Falls, nope, DeSoto falls, definitely not. Hemlock falls, Holcomb Creek, Cascade falls. I knew most of them and could rule them out right away. Of the ones I didn't, one by one I checked them off the list.

When I had run out of options, I dropped my phone in my lap. "Nothing. We need to get some help finding this place."

"I know someone that lives around there," Mila said. "She helps me sometimes when I need information."

CHAPTER · 12

Atticus didn't speak for the entire car ride. Mila and I just made small talk. For Keepers, small talk usually centered around what monsters we had fought. There seemed to always be something new and nasty coming through portals and it was good to get a heads-up on what we might run into. When the conversation lulled, my thoughts drifted to Naylet. *Wish you were here . . .* I wondered how serious she was. There was a part of me that wanted to get in the truck and go see her. It was nothing more than a pipedream. I was a Keeper of Thera. The job didn't come with vacation time. I found myself wishing for freedom, that Thera would just stay gone. I knew it wasn't going to happen though. Maybe one day Naylet would come back. Then, maybe, we could see about rekindling our relationship.

"We're here," Mila said, snapping me out of my daydream.

I looked up to see a single-story white house by the river. A simple country home, modest by modern standards, it looked to be from the late forties or early fifties. It had a rustically constructed outbuilding that looked older than the house. An old pickup and a newer sedan were parked inside.

Mila parked behind the pickup. "Atticus, wait here for me. We won't be long."

The blanket he was wrapped in nodded a little.

Mila and I headed to the front door.

Mila rang the doorbell. "Let me do the talking. She takes a bit to open up to people."

As soon as the doorbell rang a small dog started raising hell inside the house. The barking got louder as the door opened a crack. A young woman peeked through the crack. At least she looked like a young woman. She seemed more interested in me than Mila.

She eyeballed me up and down. "Who's this?"

Mila spoke softly. "This is Obie. He's a Keeper like me and a good friend. We need your help."

The door closed, muffling the yapping. I was starting to think that was her way of telling us to fuck off when the door opened again to reveal a gray werefox holding a black-and-white shih tzu. The dog growled and barked as we stepped inside the house.

"Obie, this is Jessie and Oreo," Mila said.

The dog growled in my direction. Jessie looked at me before turning to Mila. "You should've called."

"Sorry," Mila said. "It's a last minute emergency kind of thing."

Jessie shrugged. "So, what did you need?"

"We need to find a house," Mila said.

"You can look realtors up online."

"Not to buy," I said. "If we're right it's full of hunters that have been abducting people. We think it's close by."

She looked at me blankly before turning back to Mila. "Let's make it fast, I'm in the middle of a *Vampire Diaries* marathon." Jessie walked down a hallway.

"Haven't you seen it a hundred times already?" Mila asked.

"What's your point?" Jessie asked.

We followed her into an office. She put Oreo down and sat at a desk with four monitors and a computer with lights casting a blue tint on the room. I didn't know much about computers but even I could tell this was a serious setup. The computer's tower had a clear side, showing off the components inside. It looked like a piece of alien technology to me. It wasn't the only computer in the room either. The walls had numerous computers and components piled around. The room was kind of a mess, but the desk was neat and clean and looked like some kind of shrine, a place to worship at the altar of technology. In a way, it reminded me of the clubhouse in the middle of the junkyard of Morrison Salvage.

Jessie grabbed the mouse and wiggled it back and forth on a mouse-pad. The monitors blinked to life. "Tell me what you know."

"We're looking for a house. It's old and big, there's three or four stories, and it's beside a waterfall," Mila said. "Oh, and there are two bridges beside each other. One is an old stone number and the other is newer."

Jessie stopped typing when Mila mentioned the bridges. She spun around in her chair to face us. "Looks like I'll be back to my show in a few minutes."

"You know it?" Mila asked.

"The place you're looking for is about five miles upriver from here. It's an old grist mill. The waterfall was manmade. They used it to turn the wheel originally but replaced it with a generator so it makes its own power."

"What can you tell us about the owner?"

Jessie sighed. I looked over her shoulder as she pulled the property up on the computer.

She stopped typing. "*Ocupado.*"

"Sorry," I said, taking a step back.

She resumed typing. "Let's see. It looks like it was sold a few years ago to . . . a dummy corporation. I might be able to find out some more for you but it will take time. I should be able to have something for you tomorrow morning."

"There was one more thing," I said. "This may not make any sense but if I needed to look at a dark place on the internet where would I go? Dark web something or other?"

Holt had already given me input on it, but Jessie was clearly an expert. I hoped she could help me figure out what Travis was talking about.

"Yeah, the dark web is a thing. You can't just look at it, it takes a special browser. It's basically the black market online. You can buy just about anything illegal there from drugs to weapons to people."

"What about 'cryptic currency'?"

"Cryptocurrency. It's digital money."

"Is there any way to trace purchases?" I asked.

Jessie nodded. "Most people think its untraceable, but there is a ledger of transactions called a blockchain. It takes some work, but transactions can be traced."

I pulled the address label and instructions we'd picked up from the foreman and handed it to Jessie. "A guy bought a summoning ritual at the dark web place and had it delivered. Could you look up who's selling this stuff, and if possible, who's purchased from them?"

Jessie handed me her notepad. "Write down everything you know about the buyer. I'll have to start there and work my way back."

I wrote down the foreman's name, the name of his construction company, and any other details that might come in handy outside of the address she already had on the return label.

Jessie eyed the notes I had written. "Eight."

"Eight what?" I asked.

Jessie crossed her arms and leaned back in her chair. "Eight thousand dollars. You think some stranger comes into my house, starts barking orders, and I'm going to drop everything I'm doing and work for free?"

"Well no . . . I just didn't know what you were talking about," I said.

"Check back in a couple days and be ready to pay," Jessie said. "Mila knows the way out."

"Umm . . . Is there a reason you couldn't do it now?" I asked.

"Let's say I was able to look it up for you in the next five minutes. What are you going to do with that information between now and two days from now?"

"I mean . . . Well . . . Nothing I guess," I said.

"I'm a few episodes away from Elena and Damon driving the car into the mystic grill. I'm not working on anything more complicated than a bag of popcorn before then."

I scratched my head. "I don't know what that means."

"It means it's time to go," Mila said. "Can you give us the address or directions to the house so we can check it out?"

Jessie flipped to a blank page of the notepad and scribbled on it. Ripping it free from the pad she flipped her wrist, presenting the paper to me held between two fingers. The gesture was a flashy way to present the paper and simultaneously say *get out.*

"Thanks," I said, taking the paper. "I'll check back in a few days."

"With cash," Jessie added.

I followed Mila outside, passing the paper to her halfway to the car. "With any luck we'll have Holt and be heading home before morning."

"Let's not count our Keepers before they're rescued," Mila said.

We headed north. In fifteen minutes, we came to a pair of bridges. One was modern, made of concrete and steel. The other was old, made of natural stone that I'd bet was pulled out of the river it crossed.

Mila slowed the car to a crawl as we crossed the bridge. She asked Atticus, "Is this it?"

Atticus studied a large three-story house built riverside, about two hundred yards downstream from the bridges. Even from this distance I could hear the water rushing.

"That's it," Atticus said. "I'm sure of it."

I caught the smell of something burning and felt heat coming from the back seat. Heat waves and little wisps of smoke rose from Atticus.

"Deep breaths, okay?" Mila said, looking in the rearview.

Atticus nodded, inhaling deeply. He held the breath for a few seconds and blew it out. The heat dissipated slightly.

"Let's find somewhere to park and get a closer look," I said.

Mila pulled off the road out of sight of the house. "Stay here and don't catch my car on fire."

We left Atticus in the back seat. Mila stepped into the woods, out of sight of the road, and pulled her shirt off.

"What are you doing?" I asked.

"We'll have an easier time staying hidden in our animal forms," she said.

I didn't need to remove my clothes to take the form of an otter. I made the change, crawling out through the neck hole of my shirt in time to get a view of Mila au natural. Her body was all powerful curves and silky definition. She looked as if she had been carved out of marble. Statuesque perfection in a living form.

It had been a while since I'd seen a naked woman. Yes, there were some at the T.O.'s run a few months ago but in krasis the fur tends to cover things up. I was suddenly aware not only that I was staring but that she was watching me watching her.

"Like what you see?" she asked doing a little spin.

I didn't know what to say other than a stammering apology that would only make this more awkward. Instead, I scampered deeper into the woods.

"So that's what an otter looks like blushing." She chuckled.

She appeared a moment later in the form of a mountain lion. We moved closer to the house, staying as quiet as we could in the crisp autumn leaves. It was easy to stay concealed in the darkness. I could smell cigarette smoke. A figure on the porch moved lazily, the faint red dot of a cigarette floating along with him at mouth level. The red dot turned into a glow, lighting up his face before fading back to an almost imperceptible speck.

While I didn't recognize his face, I knew the body language. The way he was holding his arms close to his chest told me he held a gun. It's not completely unheard of for a guy to be hanging out on a porch with a gun in these parts. But Atticus identified the location, I doubted it was just some guy spending quality time with his rifle.

"What do you think?" Mila asked.

She was able to shift only her vocal chords, allowing her to speak as a mountain lion. I hadn't practiced that specifically, but I had worked on partial changes to be able to pull my blade out of my back in my human form. This would be the same thing only different. I concentrated on shifting my throat.

I could feel the movement of the shift as my neck changed. "It's worth a look," I said, sounding like I had just taken a hit from a helium balloon.

Mila put her head down and covered her face with her paws. She laughed. I would have told her it wasn't funny but speaking more would only encourage her. I could feel my brow furrow and the left side of my mouth raise as I waited for her to get herself under control. When she looked over at me and saw my face she started up all over again.

I made my way back to my clothes, changed into krasis, and started getting dressed. Mila followed right after.

"I'll call Hank and get the Tortured Occult up here to help out," I said, buttoning my pants.

Thera appeared beside us. "I have a job for you. Mila, since you're here you can go as well."

"Where have you been? I've been calling you," I said.

Thera looked at me with a blank expression. "I heard your calls."

"And?"

"I chose not to answer," she said.

"Can you locate Holt?" Mila asked. "Is he in that building over there?"

"I have a job for you," Thera repeated.

"My first priority is Holt," I said. "If I'm right, he's inside that house and in big trouble."

Thera ignored me and continued with her instructions. "Eirene spoke to me. There are humans hurting her children. You will go to her and stop them. Do not impose on her."

"I'll be sure not to, right after I get Holt back," I said. "That's the priority."

Electricity shot through me. My body convulsed and I fell to my knees. I looked up at Thera.

She looked down her nose at me. "I grow weary of your insolence. You have become too comfortable making demands of me. It's time you remembered your place."

I went to stand up when I was hit again. My body shot with pain and I fell, flopping like a fish as a second jolt hit me. Mila stood by and quietly watched. I couldn't blame her. Protesting would have only brought Thera's wrath on her. The pain ceased. I was able to move again. I knelt in front of Thera, holding back my anger.

"Do you have anything else to say?" Thera asked.

I didn't say anything but sat there with my head bowed.

Thera waved her arm and a portal opened in front of us. "Then go."

CHAPTER · 13

We stepped through the portal into a small clearing. We were surrounded by a jungle with dense vegetation and strange animal sounds emanating from all around us, it's what I imagined the Amazon rainforest would be like. The air felt heavy and smelled like rain. Movement in the foliage directly in front of us caught my attention. I put a hand on the handle of my blade as Mila moved a few feet to my right. A standard tactic. If something rushed us we would be ready.

A woman materialized out of the jungle. Her skin was stone gray with a mix of green foliage that matched the jungle for hair. I knew the look, it was the same way Thera appeared, when she chose to.

I dropped my hand from my blade. "Eirene?"

Mila moved toward me cautiously. She gave me a look that I recognized as anxious. I understood it, I was feeling the same way. We learned how Thera liked things done. Eirene was an unknown. How were we supposed to handle this meeting? Do we bow, kneel, or stand there looking stupid. Was there a way she wanted to be addressed and what were the consequences for breaking the rules? Was I going to say the wrong thing and end up flailing in pain again?

Eirene smiled and stepped up to me. She looked kind enough but I didn't trust her. She raised her hands to my face. I took half a step back. She saw my trepidation and paused. I relaxed a little and she placed a middle finger on each temple. A warm tingle ran from her fingers into my head; my right eye twitched involuntarily from the energy flow. When she finished with me she went to Mila. I didn't know what she had done but it didn't hurt. I gave Mila a nod. She let Eirene put her hands to her temples.

When Eirene had finished she stepped back. "Now you are as my children. Thank you for coming. I hope you will be able to put an end to the violence quickly. Your guide will be here soon."

Eirene disappeared.

"What'd ya think that meant?" Mila asked. "You are as my children."

I shrugged. "Has to be a good thing, right?"

We were left standing alone in the jungle surrounded by strange noises. There was chirping, screeching, and howling but the most alarming sound was a deep guttural thumping. *Kuh, kuh, kuh.*

Mila looked around at the jungle. "What now?"

"She said there's a guide. Maybe just wait here?"

Mila took a step closer to the jungle. "You hear that? What do you think's making all that racket?"

"Probably a lot of creatures we've never seen before. I don't want to piss off Eirene. I think it'd be smart to avoid killing as much as we can while we're here."

"Except the humans," Mila interjected.

I smiled. "Of course."

I felt a tap on my whiskers that made me wiggle my mouth. It began to rain, the pitter pat of the raindrops hitting the leaves grew into a shushing drone as if the jungle was telling us to be quiet.

I didn't mind the water. It soaked my clothes but my fur offered excellent protection. Mila, on the other hand, wasn't as comfortable. The rain soaked into her fur, weighing it down against her skin. She looked like a drowned cat, which wasn't far from the reality.

"You look miserable," I said.

"Where's that guide already?" She asked, taking shelter under one of the larger leaves.

There was a rustling in the brush. Mila and I turned to face the noise.

"Finally," Mila said.

I waited for the guide we had heard about. There wasn't any movement I could see but the jungle was thick with vegetation. This guide sure was taking their sweet time. Somewhere in the brush the same low thump sounded much closer than it had been. *Kuh kuh kuh kuh.*

Something large rushed us from behind, knocking me to the ground. I landed face down in the dirt. Something large and heavy stood on my back, pinning me to the ground. The pressure made it hard to breathe. A sharp pain stabbed into my back in multiple places. A lizard-like foot with razor sharp claws dug into the ground beside my head.

I reached back, trying to pull my blade from its sheath. The creature had it pinned to my body. I could feel the claws digging into my back and realized there wasn't much I could do about it. Mila came to the rescue. She raked her claws across the beast's face. It roared and charged her. She dodged its lunge but it spun slamming its tail into her, sending her flying into the brush. I wasn't one to lay around when there's work to be done. I got to my feet and drew my blade.

In front of me was a creature that looked like a cat with feathers and spikes on the end of its tail. While I'd intended to leave no trace, I had no intention of being disemboweled. I lunged, stabbing my blade into the beast's side. It spun, snapping at me. I jumped back, avoiding the bite. It took a few steps toward the jungle and collapsed. A second beast jumped out of the jungle, putting itself between me and the injured one. Its throat lurched like a bullfrog, making a guttural thump. *Kuh . . . kuh.* It waved its spiked tail threateningly back and forth.

As long as I could avoid its tail, I felt confident I could take it. I was used to fighting things with sharp claws and teeth. There was a rustling in the brush to my right. I took a step away. I'd have a hard time fighting off two of them at the same time. I hadn't seen Mila since she took that tail hit. If she could heal enough to give me some backup, we might have a chance.

It surprised me when an orc crashed through the brush. He stood five and a half feet tall with gray skin and a couple of large teeth sticking out from his bottom jaw. He was stocky with the thick muscular build common to orcs. He was dressed in a tunic and kilt made of some kind of woven material and carried a staff covered with intricate carvings.

He looked from me to the monsters and back to me. He jumped between us pointing his staff at my face in a threatening gesture. The staff had objects tied to the end of it with ropes that matched his clothing. A small skull, a bouquet of plants, a shiny rock, and a feather that looked like it came from one of these creatures bounced around on the end of the staff.

"Back, demon!" The orc shouted. "You shall not hurt Eirene's children."

Taken off my guard, I stepped back. It wasn't what he said, but how he said it. He wasn't speaking English, I didn't know the language, but I understood. Eirene must have given me the language when she touched me. If I could understand the language, I might be able to speak it.

I concentrated on what I wanted to say and gave it a shot. "If they don't hurt me, I won't hurt them."

The sounds that came out of my mouth were made up of long vowels and staccato grunting. I could tell by his change in expression that the orc understood me. What was weird was that I could understand what I said as well. It was mildly disorienting to fluently speak a language I didn't even know the name of.

He lowered the staff slightly. "If you know my language then you must be who I'm here to meet. I was told there were two of you."

Mila stumbled out of the brush. Her clothes were blood stained. "There is," she snarled. "Not if those beasts had their way about it."

The orc lowered his guard. He stabbed the butt of his staff into the ground. "They are leeree and one is injured. I must help her before we can continue our mission."

"Don't worry about me, I'm fine. By all means let's help the vicious predators," Mila scoffed.

She spoke in English but since she responded to what the orc had said I knew she understood and could speak his language. It also meant we had a way to speak privately. I doubted Eirene knew English, or that she planted it into his mind.

The orc knelt beside the injured leeree. The second leeree stood over him as he looked at the animal's injuries. It regarded us threateningly but didn't mind the orc's presence in the least. It was as if it was guarding both of them.

I kept my blade out and stood at a safe distance. "What's your name?"

"Krom," he said. "This injury is severe. You have a sharp claw."

"It was made by an orc like you," I said.

"Oorug."

"No, his name was Yarwor."

Krom stopped tending to the leeree and looked at me. "We are oorug, not *orc.*"

"Sounds similar enough to me," Mila said in his language.

Krom grunted his disapproval and turned back to the wounded animal. "I'll need to gather some plants for the healing ritual."

"How long's that going to take?" I asked.

"I have to gather everything and prepare the ritual," Krom said. "It will take some time, impossible to tell."

Mila was particularly pissed off after being punted into the jungle. "Just leave it and let's go. There are more important things to handle right now."

"If this one loses its mate she will become sad. A sad leeree is a dangerous leeree," Krom said. "Oorug are stewards of Eirene. It is my duty to heal this gentle creature."

I put my blade in its sheath. "We don't have time for that. Can you keep this fuckin' thing from attacking me?"

"I won't let you harm it more than you have," Krom said.

"I'm not going to hurt it. Can you just do as I ask?"

Krom stood and led the uninjured leeree to the side of the clearing. I looked over at Mila. She gave me a nod affirming she had my back. I moved forward slowly, wary the leeree would attack. I knelt beside the animal, holding my hand out over it, and began channeling energy into it. I wasn't sure it would work since I hadn't tried any of my normal abilities. The energy began to flow through my body and into the leeree. I could see pink of the animal's wound begin to disappear as the injury closed.

When the energy spilled over the animal, the healing was complete. I stood and backed away slowly. The leeree got to its feet. It turned and lurched its head at me. *Kuh.* With that, the two leeree disappeared into the jungle.

Krom looked at the blood on Mila's clothes. "How badly are you injured? Can you walk?"

"I'm fine," she said.

"Remarkable. Eirene was wise to obtain the help of such powerful demons."

"How far do we need to go?" I asked.

"Half Kuu," Krom said, walking in the direction he had come from.

"What's a Kuu?" Mila asked.

"It's the seed of a goroo tree," Krom said.

"How are we half a seed away?" I asked. "That doesn't make any sense."

Krom turned around, holding his hands about a meter apart. "A Kuu is about this big. It has a thick fibrous husk that we use to weave into clothing, ropes, nets. After the husk is removed the seed is cooked in a pit filled with coals covered in goroo leaves and buried. One Kuu is the time it takes for the Kuu seed to cook."

"So the time it will take us to get there is half the time it takes a Kuu seed to cook?" Mila asked.

Krom started walking again. "Yes."

"That clears it up," I said.

CHAPTER 14

It rained for close to an hour. After the first fifteen minutes, Mila was so soaked it looked like she'd never be dry again. We both seemed to get considerably more sour as we walked. It wasn't the rain for me, it was that I had time to think. It didn't sit right with me that Thera forced us to come here and leave Holt in trouble.

"Relax," Mila said. "You're too distracted. Just focus on the job at hand."

We had been speaking in English while we walked, mostly because I had been complaining most of the way and I didn't want Krom to hear what a whiner I was being.

"I don't get what we're doing here. Why couldn't we just come through the portal close to the folks we're supposed to handle?" I asked. "We're out here wandering through the jungle wasting time when Holt's in real trouble."

Mila put a hand on a branch in front of her and bent it out of our way. "All I'm saying is, focusing on that isn't going to get us out of here any sooner."

I stopped. "Yeah yeah . . . I know. It's just that we were right outside. We could have gone in, got him back, and put an end to people getting snatched on our own planet. It wouldn't have taken more than an hour. Instead, we had to come here to solve other peoples' problems."

"These oorug seem pretty peaceful," Mila said. "I'm not sure they could take care of themselves."

"Maybe they should learn."

"You don't mean that," she said. "You're just upset."

"Yeah, I am upset."

Mila must have been tired of my bitching because she changed the subject. "Why do you think they measure time in kuu?"

"Well, I'm sure they have days, the sun has to go down sometime doesn't it?"

She thought about it. "Maybe it's like Alaska where it's light and dark for months at a time?"

"Maybe, this thick canopy would block out sunlight either way. A sundial wouldn't work. I guess it makes sense, they would all know how long it takes kuu to cook."

"We should keep moving," Krom said. "It is dangerous here for you."

I stepped past Mila and the branch she was holding. "How much farther?"

"It's not far now," he said. "It's just ahead."

"Good, someone back home needs my help. We need to get this over with quick."

Krom looked confused. "You're showing concern for another."

"So?" I scoffed.

"You're not what I expected. Demons are notorious for viciousness. It's strange to hear one showing concern."

"We have names," I said. "I'm Obie, this is Mila."

"I am curious about your species. May I ask you some questions?" Krom asked.

"Anything to pass the time," Mila said.

"Have you killed many creatures."

"What do you consider many?" Mila asked.

Krom pondered the question. "I am unsure."

"Yes, we've both killed many," I added. "More than could be counted."

That wasn't exactly true, but it got the point across.

Krom walked quietly for a moment before posing his next question. "Are you a mated pair?"

I looked back at Mila. She had a grin running from ear to ear.

"Are you going to start blushing again?" she asked in English.

I rolled my eyes. "We aren't a mated pair."

"Do you have mates?"

Mila spoke up after I didn't answer. "Obie had one until recently. I have a few."

"Private," I said in English.

"What?" Mila smirked. "When we're done here you'll never see him again. Who do you think he's going to tell?"

"That's not really the point is it?"

Krom turned around to me. He put a hand on my shoulder. "Demon Obie, you've lost a mate. You're sad and grumpy like the leeree. It takes countless kuu for a leeree to return to itself after losing a mate as well as care from the oorug. I will show you the care of a mateless leeree."

I wanted to be mad at him but how could I when he was expressing genuine concern for me. The truth was, I was just annoyed with the whole situation.

"This is your fault," I said to Mila before turning back to Krom. "Thanks . . . I think. How much farther?"

Krom gave me a smile and a shoulder squeeze before he disappeared through the brush in front of us. "We have arrived."

I drew my blade and went in after him. I emerged through the brush expecting explosions, screaming, or gunfire. What I found was a tree branch as wide as a road. It stretched from the distance into the ground in front of us and shot back up into what looked like a new tree. A small group of oorug were gathered around. Some were braiding cords, others were cooking. Children played in the clearing around a group of adults that looked to be sitting and talking around a small fire.

Panic erupted when they saw us. They dropped whatever they were doing. Some bolted up the limb while others ran after children.

Krom waved his hands. "Don't be concerned by their hideous appearance. They were brought to us by Eirene, no need to panic."

Some of the oorug didn't slow down and continued their ascent up the branch. Others waited cautiously, unsure about Krom's claim. The children clung close to adults or peeked around their legs. They seemed to ease a little when I put my blade back in its sheath.

"Krom, where are the humans?" I asked.

He looked confused. "What are *hoomans?*"

"The demons . . . we thought you were taking us to them," Mila said.

"Come," he said, walking toward the branch. "I will show you."

The crowd of oorug moved aside leaving a path. We followed Krom up the branch. The bark of the tree was thick and knotted but the top of the branch had smooth trails worn into it from the traffic. As we cleared the tree line I could see where we were headed, a massive tree, one whose trunk stretched at least fifty yards in diameter. The trunk was straight with a few branches like the one we were standing on reaching out in different directions into the jungle. Its canopy was enormous and as we got closer I could see huts constructed onto the branches or built into the side of the trunk. We walked for twenty minutes before we got to the trunk.

Krom disappeared inside an oorug-sized hole in the trunk. Mila and I ducked to get in and found the oorug utilized the inside of the tree as well. The tree was hollow nearly to the top. Huts were built into the trunk above us. Multiple rope bridges spanned the interior. There were a lot of openings in the trunk that light came through, but it wasn't enough to light the inside of the tree. There was light from scattered candles or lamps. The closest was on a platform suspended by ropes in the middle of the tree. We followed Krom to the platform. He picked up a large shell resembling a conch shell. The end of the shell had been hollowed out and held a small flame.

Krom handed it to Mila. "If it tips the oil will spill. Stand here." He indicated the platform.

We got on and Krom pulled a rope that ran to the top of the tree. The platform started to ascend. A net full of red rocks acted as a counterweight coming down beside us. The rocks looked familiar. It took me a second to figure out why—they reminded me of Yarwor's scimitar. His blade was made out of a red metal I hadn't seen anywhere else. It made sense it came from here but metalworking seemed beyond the skills of the oorug people, at least the ones I had seen so far. Krom calling my blade a claw instead of a sword told me they didn't engage in metalworking.

"Krom, do the oorug people travel through portals to other worlds?" I asked.

Krom pulled another rope. The platform stopped with a jolt in front of a hut. Mila was caught off guard by the jolt and the lamp tipped spilling a little oil.

He tied off the rope and stepped off the platform into the hut. "It is said that long ago our people did travel. It led to great suffering so now it is forbidden."

The hut seemed to be used for storage. There were a number of what I guessed to be kuu seeds as well as ropes, shells, and other things that I didn't recognize. The hut was well organized with everything stacked neatly or held in baskets. A door on the other side of the hut led to one of the large lower limbs. The limb was about fifteen feet across with a well-worn path in the middle. Large clumps of seeds, that reminded me of grapes, hung from the branches above us.

Krom pointed off into the distance. "The demons are there."

I stepped past him and squinted. There seemed to be a hole in the jungle. The white tops of tents were visible near the center of the void.

"Looks like they made themselves at home," Mila said.

"They brought strange animals with them. The animals sleep most of the time but when they wake they roar."

"What do they do with these animals?" I asked.

"Some they ride, others they use to chew through trees. They are killing the trees to make room for their cloud huts," Krom said.

"What are they doing here?" Mila asked.

"They are capturing Eirene's children. I do not know the purpose."

"Okay, Let's get over there and put a stop to it," I said.

"It will be dark soon. We should wait until light . . . you smell wrong," Krom said. "Follow me."

He took us back to the storage hut and picked up a gourd, liquid sloshed inside it. He took the lamp from Mila and put it on a stack of seeds behind him.

He took a stopper out of the top of the gourd and began slinging the liquid on Mila and me. "It is oil of the goroo leaf. It should mask your scent."

I wiped oil out of my face. "What's the point of this again?"

"Eirene's children hunt by scent. Now you will smell like oorug and be safe. You should rub it in."

CHAPTER 15

When I was a kid in the orphanage one of my favorite things to do when I snuck out at night was to stargaze. That was back before smartphones and TVs and you could see stars all the way down to the horizon. Now, with nothing to do but wait, I lay on one of the enormous limbs of the kuu tree and looked up through the branches. Krom snored lightly, leaning against the trunk. There were two moons on this world, both were close to full which were doing a good job illuminating the jungle below. The only other light came from the camp in the distance. I could barely make out the steady rumble of a generator providing power to light up the camp like Christmas.

I could see why Krom wanted to wait until morning. The jungle was alive with howls and screeches. If I'd had my druthers I would have headed straight to the camp. I had no idea, however, what other dangerous creatures were out there. Even covered in goroo oil, I wouldn't feel good about moving through the jungle at night.

I was worried about what was happening to Holt right now. Hunters only had two motivations, hate and dust, neither of which required their victims to be alive. They were normally a shoot first kind of bunch. I couldn't figure out why this group changed strategies to capture rather than kill. Then there was the tar, that meant magic. This wasn't just a couple hunters working on their own. They were organized. Professional. That worried me as much as anything. One thing I was sure about, any harm that came to him would be on Thera. I just wanted to be home to handle it. Instead, I had all night to lay around doing nothing. Having nothing to focus on besides my thoughts wasn't making the situation any better.

I didn't even have Mila to talk to. She had gotten bored and decided to look around. The oorug were a peaceful people, stewards of Eirene. They posed no threat to us or anything higher on the food chain than a kuu seed from what I could see. It made sense to me now why Thera ordered us to come here—not that I was happy about it. These people were wholly unequipped to handle violence. The threat on this world was from the animals that lived here. Firearms alone would make conquering this entire planet a cake walk.

My thoughts turned to Naylet. She would normally have been my confidant in times like this but she was gone, too. I stuck my hand into my pocket and pulled out the postcard. It had gotten a little frayed around the edges at some point, probably in the fight with the leeree. I looked at the picture on the front and flipped it over. *Wish you were here.* I ran a finger over the words, feeling the indentations in the paper. It may sound strange, but lying there with just a postcard and the stars I felt closer to her than I had in a long time even though we'd never been farther apart.

Her handwriting looked different than it had before the attack. I couldn't put my finger on what was different about it, it was just a little off, as if it were a good forgery. They say you can tell things about a person's personality in their handwriting. If there was actually anything to that I wondered what it said about Naylet. Was she mostly the same or was it just muscle memory? That's when I made the decision. I had to find out. When I put an end to these hunters, got back to Earth, and rescued Holt, I'd track down Naylet. Maybe go for a cup of coffee.

"What's that?" Mila asked.

I tilted my head back. She walked out of the tree onto the branch past Krom.

"A postcard," I said, wondering exactly how much I wanted to tell her. "It's from Naylet."

Mila sat beside me. "Oh, she's sending you postcards?"

"A few here and there. Just to let me know where she's going kind of thing."

"Can I see it?" She asked, holding out her hand.

I hesitated before handing the card to her. She read it and with a light *hum* she passed it back.

"What?"

She shrugged. "Nothing, It's not my place."

"No. What?" I asked. "If you got something to say spit it out."

"Well, it's just . . . Have you considered she's just telling you what you want to hear?"

I gave her a squinted glare. "What do you mean?"

"You're paying all the bills for her trip, right? What happens to her if you decide to stop?"

"You think she's using me."

"I think it's a possibility. How much have you actually talked to her since she . . . got better? Does she know you well enough to actually miss you?"

I didn't have a good answer, but Naylet wasn't using me as Mila was suggesting. You can't steal what's freely given. I put no conditions on the money. There was no reason for Naylet to think she had to manipulate me into paying. I suppose it's possible she could be hedging her bets. It wasn't something the old Naylet would do, but it accentuated the question I already had. How different was she?

"Look," she said, "I'm saying you should see what's out there. Stop focusing so much on the past. Have some fun."

"I think it's going to work out in the long run," I said, shoving the postcard back in my pocket. "It sounds cheesy but I really believe we're soulmates. It's fate or something."

Mila tilted her head and pursed her lips. A pitying expression I didn't much care for. "In my experience fate is wholly unreliable."

I changed the subject. "You've been gone a while. Anything interesting out there?"

Mila shrugged. "I explored the tree. You can get almost to the very top. It's like standing on a skyscraper."

"I'll have to check that out," I lied.

"The sun will be up soon," Mila said.

I propped myself on my elbows. "And how do you know that?"

She pointed to the horizon. "You can see it."

She was right, the sky was beginning to lighten.

"What d'ya think? About one sixteenth kuu until the sun's up?"

She laughed. "Let's just say *soon.*"

"Fair enough," I said. "I don't think measuring time in vegetables is going to catch on."

Mila got to her feet. "Technically, it's a fruit I think."

"Same difference."

She walked over to Krom, giving him a nudge with her paw. He snorted in surprise and opened his eyes.

He ran a hand over his face. "What's the matter?"

"The sun's coming up," I said. "It's time to go."

He grunted and got to his feet. "Almost."

"I've been thinking," Mila said. "You told us that they capture Eirene's children. How do they do that?"

"Magic. They have long sticks. When they point the sticks at something it falls asleep," Krom said.

"Do the sticks make noise?" I asked.

Krom shook his head. "Not those sticks. They do have thunder sticks but those bring death."

I could see the sorrow in his face. I wondered if some of the oorug had been killed but I wasn't going to ask.

"How many demons are there?" Mila asked.

"About fifteen," Krom said. "A big group goes out to hunt with a few staying behind with the cloud huts."

"How long will it take to get to the demons?" I asked.

"Two *kuu*," Krom said.

Mila bent over, picked up my blade, and handed it to me. "We better get started."

I could feel her hands on the blade, and I expected to be skeeved out by it but I wasn't. It didn't bother me at all and that caught me off guard. She must have realized something was up when she caught me looking at her.

"What's that face mean?" she asked.

I didn't know what it meant. She was the first person to touch my blade without making my skin crawl. I didn't know what it meant or how I felt about it.

I shook my head and looked away. "Nothing. It's just . . . nothing."

CHAPTER · 16

Krom moved through the jungle in a carefree stroll as if he were walking through a park. It was clear the oorug were outside the food chain, at peace with all life on this world. I didn't share his jovial attitude. Something about watching Mila getting clubbed into the jungle yesterday gave me a little more apprehension about our jungle stroll. The oil Krom threw on us smelled like a mix of coconut and sage. I was skeptical that it would actually work, but after walking for hours we weren't attacked once so it must be doing something. We saw a number of strange creatures on the way, some of which looked predatory, but none gave us more than a sniff and a passing glance.

After about four hours of walking we came to a river roughly thirty feet across. The water was deep enough that I couldn't see the bottom even though the water would have looked pristine except for some cans and plastic that had found its way into the water.

"The cloud huts are close," Krom said.

I knelt on the riverbank and splashed cool water on my face. It felt great after the trek through the jungle. "I can see their—" The oorug word for trash or litter wasn't coming to me. I thought I was just having a hard time thinking of it but then I realized the words didn't exist. The closest thing was a phrase I wasn't sure applied but it was the best I could do. "Discarded seeds."

Krom shook his head. "Those are not seeds."

"They're not," I agreed. "We'll clean it up after we get rid of the demons."

"Why don't you head back to the tree," Mila said. "This could get dangerous and . . . Let's just say your people don't seem suited to violence."

"I'm your guide," he said. "I need to protect Eirene's children from you and you from them."

"Suit yourself," I said. "I'm gonna look around a little, get a feel for things."

"I'll look around this side of the river," Mila said.

I took the form of an otter, shrinking to a fraction of my size in krasis. Since I didn't undress first, I ended up inside a pile of clothes. I felt something poking me through my shirt. Climbing out through the neck hole of my shirt I looked up to see Krom poking at my clothes with his staff. It was clear he had never seen a shifter before.

"Eirene's blessings," Krom exclaimed. "Do you have this power?" he asked, turning to Mila.

"Yes, but I'm a much scarier creature," she said, peeling off her clothes.

She took the form of a mountain lion and headed for the trees. I gave them a squeak, and walked to the river bank. The water was about eight feet deep and thirty feet across with a swift but manageable current. I headed downstream first, I felt like taking it easy after the hike. I could rest up on the way down and fight the current on the way up or get out and walk if it came to it. I hadn't gone far when I found the first sign of people. A beer can was trapped between a rock and the shore. Next, I spotted some brown plastic stuck on a root a little farther downstream. I swam to it and picked it up. It had MRE stamped across the front.

"Meal, Ready to Eat," I squeaked. "Menu one, chili with beans."

I gave the open end of the package a sniff. Any trace of the chili had been washed out of the bag; it had been here a while. Swimming farther downstream, I found a few more pieces of garbage. I didn't see any sign of the camp besides trash, and considering the direction the water was flowing, it would put camp upstream. I turned around. It took a lot more work to get back to where I had left Krom. When I got to the spot, I saw him disappearing into the jungle. He carried our clothes. I figured his plan was to stay hidden to make sure we weren't discovered. Smart.

I swam farther upstream, the litter growing more dense as I went. Around the next bend I heard people talking. I climbed out of the river and followed the voices into the jungle. I found a man standing beside a woman kneeling over something. I couldn't see the woman clearly through the vegetation. The man had a light auburn beard, a black baseball cap with a four leaf clover, and gray coveralls. He had a rifle that looked to fire darts as well as a pistol on his hip.

"Heather, I really think we should go back," the man said. "We're not supposed to be out here alone."

She fished around in her pocket for something. "Relax, Jarod, this area's clear, and address me as Professor or Professor Bennett."

"Sorry, Professor, but if that was true then the trap wouldn't have been sprung," Jarod said.

"Cleared of anything dangerous," the woman corrected. She held a recorder to her mouth. "Subject is one half meter long. Body is gray in color with a dark green tail. Four light green stripes run from head to tail, resembling a five lined skink from the southeastern United States." She stopped the recorder. "Alright, let's bag it."

Jarod hesitated. "Should I . . . I don't know. Shoot it or something?"

"I don't want the specimen more damaged than it already is," the professor said.

Jarod stood. "The trap's crushed it pretty good. It's going to suffer being put in a bag and carried back to camp like that," he said.

She stood and faced him. "You're not being paid to think or care about these creatures. I'm the one with the doctorate in zoological medicine and you're just an overpaid porter. While I'm sure your GED is really paying off, if I tell you to carry something try not to think too much and just do as you're told."

Jarod pursed his lips and nodded.

I snuck forward to get a better look. The woman wore coveralls that matched Jarod's. It must be a uniform. She had blonde hair pulled back in a ponytail. She didn't look like a professor to me. Maybe that's why she made such a point about Jarod using the title.

She was hunched over a large lizard caught in what looked like a giant rat trap. It had snapped across the lizard's hindquarters. I was sure the trap had broken the animal's back and crushed its organs. It would die for sure if I didn't help. I wasn't going to let them take the animal back to their camp in any condition. I'd wait for them to open the trap, then I could move in, heal it, and deal with these humans. Not necessarily in that order. I backed away slowly, changed to krasis, and drew my blade. When Jarod opened the trap, I charged forward. He stood up with a writhing lizard in one hand just as I got to him. I ran my sword through his stomach and threw a shoulder into his chest. The impact made him fly off into the brush, dropping the lizard.

I knelt, holding a hand over the injured lizard and channeled healing energy into it. In a few seconds it fully recovered. A gunshot rang out. The bullet whizzed just to my right. The lizard took off into the jungle and I dove to my left. The second shot missed high as I scurried on all fours into the bushes. The gun kept firing and I kept moving, getting glimpses of the professor through the leaves. She didn't seem to be very comfortable with a pistol. She wasn't holding it correctly, exaggerating the recoil. She was more throwing bullets in my direction than shooting at me. When I got as close as I could, I charged her. I came out of the brush swinging my blade at the hand holding the gun. The blade cut through cleanly, sending a severed hand and pistol falling to the ground. I changed the momentum of the blade, bringing it low to hit her legs. I cut through one and nicked the other. She fell forward with a gasp. I drove the blade into her back and twisted it to finish her off.

It happened so fast I didn't realize what had happened until it was over. I hadn't intended to kill both of them. I wanted one alive for questioning. Krom was a fine guide but didn't understand the technology well enough to be of much help. I needed to know exactly what I was up against. I wiped my blade on the professor's shirt to clean off the blood.

Something crashed through the brush, headed in my direction. I turned to face the noise and flexed my hand around the handle of my blade, ready for whatever was about to arrive.

Mila exploded through the vegetation, skidding to a stop in front of me. "You alright? I heard the shooting."

I relaxed the grip on my blade. "Nothing I couldn't handle."

"Looks like I missed all the fun," Mila said, looking at the professor's body.

A wheezing sound drifted from the bushes. I pulled branches aside to discover Jarod wasn't dead after all. He had one hand on his belly where I had run him through. Blood trickled from his mouth. His chest heaved irregularly. He didn't have long, without help he would die. I knelt over him, tossed his pistol away, and put a hand over his wound, channeling energy into him.

"Aren't we here to stop them?" Mila asked.

I nodded. "We need information on the camp. You're not scared are ya?"

"We can always kill him later I guess."

His breathing eased as the energy healed his injuries. When the energy flowed over him I took my hand back. He opened his eyes and jumped with surprise. He looked over at the professor's body, then to his rifle lying a few feet away, then back to me.

"We need your help. You can come with us and live, or I'll make it as quick and painless as I can," I said, placing my blade against his neck. "Your call."

CHAPTER 17

"Why did you bring a demon here?" Krom asked. "I thought you were supposed to get rid of them."

"We will get rid of him and all the others," I said. "I need information and he's going to give it to me."

Jarod sat against a tree. Of course, he couldn't understand a word of what we were saying and I liked it that way. He sat perfectly still. It was probably because Mila was standing over him, giving him the stink eye. We hadn't said more than a few words to him since we captured him. I'm sure he was wrestling with the uncertainty of the situation. I didn't care.

Krom crossed his arms. "I don't see why the demon would help."

I gave him a smile. "You don't understand the demons like I do. Did you forget, I'm a demon, too. Oh, since I need him alive, can you douse him with the goroo oil?"

Krom pulled a gourd from his belt and scowled as he unceremoniously doused Jarod. "I feel I should voice my displeasure. This is against our mission and a waste of oil."

Jarod jumped when the first shot of oil hit his face. "What the hell? This an exorcism or something?"

"It'll keep animals from biting your face off," I said. "You might want to rub it in."

He hesitated at first but must have figured it was worth a shot because he started rubbing the oil into his hair and skin. "I'll do it but I won't like it."

"Nobody cares what you like," Mila said.

When Krom had finished, he backed away from Jarod, pulled out some kuu pieces, and ate. With both of my companions thoroughly displeased, I could turn my attention back to the mission.

I sat beside Jarod. "Let's get down to it."

"How is it you speak my language?" Jarod asked.

"Because I'm from Earth, you idiot," I said. "Now it's your turn to answer some questions. You can start with who you work for."

"Doctor Tsukimora," he said.

"Details."

"I really don't know much. I was barely scraping by as a truck driver when I found out about this job. It was a friend of a friend kinda thing. It sounded good, too good to be honest, but I have a daughter to take care of so I was open to it." Jarod held out his right arm. There was a tattoo that said HAILEY in large letters with a date underneath. I did some rough math in my head, his daughter would be about six years old. "It seemed a little strange to be honest, but the pay was too good to pass up. Three months away would make me more than I could make five years driving a truck so I signed up. Things got weird after that. I've only met doctor Tsukimora once when I was hired and seen him in passing a couple times."

"What's he look like?" Mila asked.

Jarod waggled his head a little to shake recollection free. "Short hair, he's always wearing suits, he's . . . Just a guy. He looks like a Wall Street type."

"Where's this facility at?" I asked.

"I really don't know exactly. Northwest Georgia somewhere. There's a giant old house by a river. It's not really a house anymore though. They're powering the place with hydropower from the river. The house itself is normal enough but there's a whole underground complex they added on underneath. I don't have access to most of it."

That sounded like the house Mila and I had been staking out. Further proof that if Thera had just let me do my job this would all have been over with already. It was frustrating to say the least.

"What about the team here?" I asked. "Tell me everything you know."

"There were twenty-five of us when we got here. Setting up camp was hell. We lost six the first day before we could get the fence set up. The animals here . . . hey, they're no joke. Our mission was to capture them alive and get them ready to take back to Earth. Don't ask me what for. The first time they left camp to try and catch something they lost another three. They changed tactics. Now, if it looks dangerous, they shoot first. The traps turned out to be more reliable so they focused on those. They set the traps and wait in camp until the sensors indicate one has been triggered. Then they go out and see what they caught."

"You said there's a fence?"

Jerod nodded. "You've seen *Jurassic Park?* You know those big electric fences they keep around the dino pens? It's like that."

Mila asked, "How's it powered?"

"Solar and batteries with a generator backup," he said. "There's a gate that's electrified that has to be shut off before it's opened or closed."

"What kind of contact is there with Earth?" I asked.

"None. They're supposed to open a portal to Earth in two days to move the things we catch. They do it on a schedule. We are supposed to be able to open one for an emergency but that won't happen now."

"Why's that?"

"You killed the person who knew how to do it. There's an instruction manual but most of the people left . . . Let's just say I don't feel good about our chances of relying on them to get home."

"Have you sent any animals to Earth already?" Mila asked.

"We sent six or seven a couple days ago. They were moved into pens right on the other side of the portal."

Mila crossed her arms. "Which is it, six or seven?"

Jarod shrugged. "My job is equipment, not livestock."

I nodded. "So here's where we're at. We were sent here to put an end to your expedition. We're going to do that first. Then we're going to get all the animals you stole back. I just have one more question for you . . . What are you willing to do to see Hailey again?"

Jarod looked away from me into the jungle and pursed his lips. "All we've got is each other. I'm here so she can have a better life than I did. I'll do whatever it takes."

"I like you, Jarod. I'm not going to lie, I can't guarantee you'll make it but I am your best chance. I can open a portal to Earth. We can help each other get home."

"I'm not stupid," he said. "You're not going to just let me go."

I knelt before him. "On this world, you're right, but on Earth you're just another guy."

Jarod nodded. "What choice do I have really?"

"What choice do you have," I agreed.

"A word," Mila said.

We walked away as not to be overheard, which turned out to be unnecessary.

"What are you doing?" she said in Oorug.

"What do you mean?"

"Well, you got this guy for information and now you're planning to take him back to Earth? Just let him go?"

"He could be useful, and if he helps us are we supposed to just turn on him?"

"We aren't turning on anyone," she said, crossing her arms. "He's one of the bad guys, remember?"

"He seems like a normal guy to me. It could be anybody sitting there. It just happened to be Jarod this time."

Mila furrowed her brow. "Where's your head at?"

"Right here, getting this job done as quick as possible so we can get home."

CHAPTER · 18

The trees and brush had been cleared thirty feet around the camp, leaving vegetation in place to rot. It served its purpose of providing a clear view of the surrounding area. Jarod was right when he said it was something out of *Jurassic Park.* The camp had cables running the perimeter, an enormous electric fence. The wires appeared to be about two feet apart, enough for Mila and me to slide under safely. The only clear path inside was the gate. A guard tower was erected by a front gate. In the tower, a single person armed with a rifle watched the jungle around the camp. I wouldn't want to try to charge into that camp. The electric fence aside, I'd bet dollars to doughnuts the shooting would start before we made it halfway across the clearing. Even without the camp's security, I didn't want to attack fifteen armed people. I was good, Mila would say she's better, but that's a lotta guns. The first thing to do was split them up.

"Jarod, how long does it take them to get to the farthest trap from camp?" I asked.

"Between loading the vehicles and drive time, about thirty minutes," he said. "They found some game trails they've been using as roads. Its about a mile up river."

I cocked my head to the side. "By upriver you mean the trap is beside the water?"

"Yeah, they found a place where the trail crosses the river. It's a natural bottleneck so a great place for a trap."

"That'll do." I mumbled to myself.

"You're planning a jungle ambush then?" he asked.

"No, I'm going to draw them out. When they're gone you'll kill the power to the fence and Mila and I'll clear the camp."

Jarod shifted uncomfortably. "How am I going to do that from out here?"

"Obviously you're not," I said. "When they leave, you walk up to the front gate and get them to let you in. As soon as you can you turn off the power to the fence. We'll handle the rest."

I looked over at Mila. She was sitting with Krom listening to our conversation. I could tell she was as excited about the plan as Jarod was.

Jarod was talking but I hadn't been listening. ". . . and where do I tell them I've been this whole time?"

"You have an hour to figure it out. Just remember, the best lies have a touch of truth to them." I went and sat beside Mila leaving Jarod out of earshot.

"You don't think we should have come up with a plan together?" she asked.

I shot her a smile. "That's not the plan. When he get's their attention focused on the gate we'll go in under the fence around back. Unless you have a better idea?"

"Why not just tell him that?"

"Let's call it plan B. If we can't get in then maybe he can kill the power and we have another shot. That way I don't have to go over what he should do in every scenario."

She crossed her arms. "What if they catch him?"

"What do you care? You're team 'kill Jarod' remember? He's not growing on you is he?"

"No," she scoffed. "Let's just get this done."

I took off my clothes and hung my shirt on a stick on the riverbank. I slipped out through the jungle alone and found the trail they had been using. The tires had ripped up the ground leaving a trail that was impossible to miss. I followed it ignoring any path that looked like it would take me away from the river. Eventually I found the trap just off the side of the trail by the riverbank. It wasn't complicated, just a bear trap with a transmitter. I found a branch sturdy enough to do the job. Once I tripped it the clock started ticking. I was sure I could make it back before they did but I needed to get there with enough time to spare. I knew from experience that I could swim about nine miles an hour. It should take me about six minutes to swim it. That was the best case scenario. Rivers weren't straight.

I stabbed the branch into the trap. Its jaws snapped shut biting into the wood. I ran for the river. I jumped from the bank in krasis and made the change in mid air hitting the water as an otter. I wove my way around the rock and branches swimming as fast as I could downstream following the twists and turns of the river. I was aware of the occasional creature in the water. Vibrations in my whiskers gave away their position. I didn't know if they were a threat or not, I didn't stop to check. I swam until I saw my shirt on the bank and got out hoping I had some time to catch my breath. I changed to krasis and got dressed. Mila, Krom, and Jarod were right where I left them watching as the camp, huddled on the edge of the clearing.

"How're we looking?" I asked.

They should be leaving any minute now," Jarod said.

I sat beside Mila to wait.

"Have any trouble?" she asked.

I shook my head. "Nah, it was a nice swim."

The gates swung open. Two vehicles loaded with people and

equipment rolled out. I counted the people on the vehicles as they passed. I wasn't sure on the exact number—it was either nine or ten—leaving four or five minding the camp. That should be easy enough to deal with.

"You clear on what to do?" I asked.

"I got it," Jarod said. "Relax."

Jarod backed away slowly, disappearing into the jungle.

Mila had a sour look on her face. I was pretty sure I knew what she was going to say. "What? What's the face?"

"I've said it before," she said without taking her eyes off the camp. "It's a bad idea to trust this guy. I don't think this is going to work out the way you think."

"I agree with Mila. We can't trust a demon," Krom butted in.

"We're demons, remember?" I said.

"You're not like those though," he said with a flick of his fingers in the direction of the camp.

"Look, if he believes that we are going to kill everyone before the portal opens again then he'll help us."

"But if he thinks his chances are better with them then he'll tell them all about us and this'll get a lot harder," Mila said.

I shook my head. "Nah, then we'll just go to plan C."

Mila and Krom both looked at me and said in unison, "What's plan C?"

"In five minutes we're going to know where Jarod's loyalty lies. If things don't come up in our favor we go after the group that went to check the trap. It will be harder but doable," I said. "Then we use the cars to crash through the gate and finish off the camp."

Mila nodded slowly, considering. "Alright, that could work."

"Will you be able to control their animals?" Krom asked. "Those *cars* look like nasty beasts."

I considered how to explain machines to him. There wasn't vocabulary to do it justice in the oorug language. "It's false life," I said. "They don't have a mind of their own and only do what someone tells them."

He looked confused but let it go.

Jarod ran out of the jungle, looking panicked. Shouting rose from the camp.

He made it to the gate and bent forward resting his hands on his knees. "Let me in," he wheezed.

"We thought you were dead," the man in the tower shouted. "We found the professor out there cut to pieces. What the hell happened?"

Jarod sounded panicky. "Damn it, Arvidson, there's something after me. Open the fucking gate!"

Jarod looked around the jungle nervously while they shut off the fence and swung the gate open. I had to give it to him, he was a good actor—*if* he was acting.

"You ready?" Mila asked.

"Yep," I said, "Let's do it."

We worked our way around to the backside of the camp opposite the tower. Mila and I changed into our animal forms. All Jarod had to do was keep the guards distracted as we made our approach. It shouldn't be hard as they all would want to hear about what happened to him.

While the trees they cut down made for open viewing, they also gave us a way to sneak up to the camp. We worked our way through the debris, staying low to avoid detection. When we got to the wire I could hear the light buzz of power running through it. I pressed my body against the dirt and slid forward until I was clear. Mila followed my lead. When we had both made it through safely we changed to krasis.

A tent gave us concealment and a chance to devise a plan of attack. I peeked around the edge of the tent. Jarod stood with four people with their backs to us; Arvidson in the tower split his attention between what was going on inside the camp and his responsibility to watch outside.

"When the guy in the tower looks away we'll charge," I whispered. "I'll go for the tower."

I drew my blade. I looked around the tent again. Arvidson was watching the discussion. As soon as he turned away I charged. I ran to the left of the group toward the tower. They must have heard our footsteps thumping on the ground because they turned just before we got to them.

Panic erupted in the group and they fumbled with weapons. I gave the one closest to me a blade in the gut. I didn't stop running. Arvidson turned to see me charging the tower. He raised his rifle and fired and I jumped to the left. The bullets slammed into the ground. I threw my blade at him. He used his rifle as a shield, deflecting it.

I leapt onto the ladder, got my footing, and jumped to the platform, landing with my arms on the edge and feet dangling off. It only had enough space for one person to stand comfortably. I steadied myself with a foot on the ladder. He brought the rifle to bear. I grabbed the barrel and shoved it to the side. He fired again. The noise turned my hearing into little more than a loud ringing. I pulled the rifle free and tossed it off the tower.

He wasn't ready to lay down and die just yet. He started kicking me in the head. I climbed onto the platform. I gave him a shot to the gut that stunned him. I got a handful of shirt with one hand and a leg with the other. I tossed him onto the electric fence. Sparks erupted. He landed with a thud and didn't move.

I looked back to see Mila, claws buried deep in a man's throat. A quick tug and he collapsed, holding the gaping wound while his life slipped away. Jarod stayed out of the fight.

"You alright?" I called down.

Mila nodded. "Took one in the arm. I've had worse."

Jarod stepped forward. "We need to hurry. They'll be back soon."

CHAPTER • 19

We sabotaged the generator and destroyed the batteries. I didn't want the fence up and running when we came back to finish the job. Krom and Jarod helped Mila and me carry the bodies and all the ammunition we could find into the jungle. We moved out of sight and waited by the equipment we had stolen.

While we waited, Jarod looked through the crates. "Maybe we should use some of this, it could come in handy."

"Keepers don't use guns all that much," Mila said, flashing the razor sharp claws on the ends of her fingers. "We have weapons built in."

"What the hell's a Keeper?" Jarod asked.

I kept my eyes on the camp when I answered. "Don't worry about it."

"I'm going to grab some food and stuff," Jarod said.

It hadn't occurred to me that he hadn't eaten since we captured him. He was probably starving. I gave him a dismissive wave.

We only had a few minutes to spare before I heard the rumble of engines. The two vehicles stopped in front of the open gate, unsure what had happened. I watched them drive forward with their guns pointing in all directions, ready for anything. Anything wouldn't be coming for them for a bit though.

A couple hours more and the sun went down, shrouding the jungle in darkness. It was different being in the jungle at night. The noises we heard from the top of the kuu tree were now surrounding us and we didn't have the luxury of elevation.

"Are you sure it's safe out here?" Jarod asked, taking the last bite of a power bar he had looted from the supplies.

He had filled up a knapsack and was smart enough to put the wrapper back into it when he was finished.

"He's asking if it's safe," Mila translated to Krom.

Krom shrugged. It may not be safe but this had gone on long enough. We were ending this tonight. I had things to tend to at home.

We waited and watched. We had all night. Without power the camp was relying on flashlights and a few lanterns positioned by the gate so they could see a threat coming. They must have decided to take shifts rather than keep everyone up until the portal was opened. After a few hours I heard snoring.

"Ready?" Mila asked.

"It's now or never," I replied. "The two of you stay here, we'll be back."

Again we took animal forms and worked our way to the edge of the fence. We slipped under the now dead wires and changed to krasis behind some crates behind the tents. Mila and I swapped some hand gestures to work out that she would take the right tent and I would take the left one.

I peeked inside. There were ten cots set up in two neat rows. Most were empty, a few had equipment stowed on them. I counted six people sleeping or at least laying down. A couple snored lightly, one was gobbling air like a chainsaw. They all either had guns draped across their chest or propped beside their cots. With so many in here I doubted there was anyone in Mila's tent.

I moved up to the closest cot and looked down at the man sleeping there. I realized I hadn't thought through how I was actually going to dispatch them without waking anyone up or alerting the guards. I thought about holding him down and cutting his throat. This wasn't some fiction novel, it was the real world. When you cut a throat they do die quickly but not immediately the way you see in the movies. They have ten or fifteen seconds to fight for life. In my experience, they fight hard. That meant thrashing and gurgling as they choked on their blood before they blacked out.

I may be able to get through a couple of them before they woke someone up but there was no way to get through all six without someone figuring out something was up. On the other hand, I couldn't just stand there all night. I got tired of thinking and worrying. Instead of trying to be quiet, I moved to the front of the tent and drew my blade.

I struck the first cot and moved toward the back, taking one swing to each cot as I went. I was on the third before the first two start making noise. The last one woke up and managed to prop himself up on his elbows before he got his.

I went out the back of the tent and ducked behind a crate. Mila was waiting there for me.

"What the hell was that?" she whispered. "I thought you were going to do it quietly."

"What about me makes you think I'm a ninja?" I jerked my head at the other tent. "Have any trouble?"

"Empty."

"Let's split up," I whispered. "I'll take this way."

"Jesus, they're all dead!" Someone shouted from inside the tent.

There wasn't much light so I wasn't worried about being silhouetted against the canvas. What I hadn't counted on was how trashy the camp was. I suppose I shouldn't be surprised considering how much garbage was in the river. I had unwittingly stumbled into the dump. Clanking from cans and swooshing from MRE bags gave away my position.

"There's something back here!" The man shouted before spraying rounds through the tent in my direction.

"Damn it, cease fire!" Another man shouted. "We don't have rounds to waste. Don't shoot until you have a clear shot."

"It's right there, behind the tent," the first man said.

Another man barked an order: "Get back behind the barricade!"

Barricade . . . I didn't like the sound of that. I'd rather get this guy before he was under cover. I stepped around the trash as quietly as I could and moved up beside the tent. I peeked around the side to see the vehicles pulled beside each other with the gaps between them blocked with crates and equipment. The one who had shot at me was backing away from the front of the tent. He was only about eight feet away but hadn't spotted me. After a few steps he turned to run.

I charged, grabbing him by the back of the neck and driving my blade into his back. I guess they weren't concerned about their comrade, or maybe they figured he was already a goner, because a fraction of a second after I stepped out they opened fire.

It turns out people make inconsistent shields. Unless the bullets hit bone they go right through and sometimes the bone doesn't stop them either. The bullets tore through the man's body as I pulled him back to the tent. Some were stopped when they hit my blade but others made it through. Pain shot through my body.

I jumped into the tent, pulling the man in with me. We fell to the ground inside with a thud. I pushed him off of me. He'd gotten the worst of it and was already dead. As soon as we disappeared through the tent flaps the shooting stopped. I could see the flashlights bathing the front of the tent as they searched for any sign of what happened to me. I'd been shot in my left arm, both legs, and more to the body than I cared to count. I coughed up some blood and I knew one of my lungs was hit. It was hard to breathe, and I hurt all over. I hoped I had a few minutes to rest. I laid down in the dirt and closed my eyes. Warmth tingled as my body began to push out the bullets and repair the damage.

"The fuck was that?' someone said from the direction of the lights.

Someone else chimed in. "You think we got it?"

"Nothing could've lived through that," the first one replied.

I lay still and healed. I figured if I didn't move then maybe they would come see if they got me. That would give Mila an opportunity to attack.

Fortunately, or unfortunately depending how you look at it, they stayed behind cover. It gave me plenty of time to heal but it meant we would have to go to them. Whoever went first wasn't going to make it, maybe neither one would. We would heal of course but it would hurt. Not exactly something to volunteer for. What other option did we have though? Stay behind cover for the next day and hope they all fell asleep or the jungle killed them? I had the time to wait but Holt didn't. I needed to find Mila.

When my body had healed enough, I stayed low and crawled out the back. I found Mila sitting behind the other tent. She was laid back in a casual pose, looking as if she was at a park on a Sunday afternoon rather than in an alien world full of things that wanted to kill us.

I sat beside her. "Got any bright ideas?"

"I think our best bet is to wait them out."

I was afraid she would say that. "We don't have time to wait."

"Then we need some way to stop bullets," Mila said.

"Maybe we could get the generator and use it as a shield?"

Rustling on the other side of the electric fence got our attention. Mila crouched, going from *a day at the park* to *what's about to jump out and eat my face.* Jarod crawled under the fence, dragging a knapsack behind him.

"What the hell are you doing here?" I asked.

He looked confused. "What? I thought we were doing this?"

"I told you to wait."

"No, you said a bunch of stuff in whatever the hell language that is and then left."

I guess we'd forgotten to switch to English. He'd just have to crawl back. We didn't have time to babysit in the middle of a gun fight.

"What's going on?" he asked.

"They're holed up behind the cars. Can't get to them," Mila said.

Jarod fished around in the knapsack and pulled out a grenade. "Will this help?"

I was a little dumbstruck. "Where'd you get that?"

"From the supplies," he said innocently.

"I thought you were getting food," I said.

Jarod nodded. "Food and stuff. Grenades are in the 'and stuff' category."

"That'll work," Mila said. "Obie and I will move to the sides. Give us thirty seconds to get in position and throw it. Just don't miss."

"I have two," he said, pulling out a second grenade. "Should I use both?"

"I was skeptical at first but you're really growing on me," Mila said with a smile. "As a person."

"Okay, whatever," I said. "Thirty seconds and throw them both."

I counted in my head as I got into position. I had counted to twenty-seven when I heard metal on metal of a grenade hitting a car followed a second later by a *thunk* of a grenade on dirt. I couldn't tell exactly where they had landed but I wasn't going to step out to look.

After the first explosion the screaming started. I saw people run from behind cover. I took off after them. The second grenade exploded. It turns out that grenade had landed on my side of the car. The two people that had come out had taken the brunt of the blast but I still caught a lot of shrapnel.

I fell, getting a face fill of dirt. Everything was quiet for a second before a shadow crossed my vision. I could feel someone standing over me. I rolled over and opened my eyes expecting Mila but found a stranger instead. He pointed his rifle at me, I closed my eyes tight as gunfire erupted. I expected to black out almost immediately. Instead, I didn't feel anything but warm blood sprinkling onto my fur and whiskers. I opened my eyes to see a hole in the man's chest. He collapsed on top of me. Mila stood behind him with a shotgun.

CHAPTER · 20

"Has the demon not served its purpose?" Krom asked. "Should he not be eliminated?"

I sighed. "I still need his help to dismantle the demon structures. The things here are still dangerous. I need to get them back to our world."

Krom sat and crossed his legs. "Don't expect me to like it."

Jarod was working on taking down the camp but must have noticed Krom's tone and body language. "What's his problem?"

I smiled. "He thinks we should kill you."

Jarod paused, not finding the humor in it, and went about his task.

We found garbage bags in the camp's equipment, not that they appeared to know how to use them. I spent hours pulling litter out of the river. It was actually the most fun I'd had since I'd gotten here. I hauled the trash back to camp. Jarod and Mila had made good progress on packing up the camp. I helped dismantle the electric fence and put all the equipment and bodies in a big pile.

When we had everything ready, I used a clawed finger to draw a circle in the dirt. It was the same one I had scratched into the dash of my truck when we followed the Queen through the portal to the demon world. I would subconsciously trace my finger over it sometimes when being taxied around by Holt. The end result was that I could draw it blindfolded with both hands tied behind my back. The incantation had been harder to memorize but with a little practice I'd managed it. I decided I never wanted to be in the situation again where I was trapped on another world with no way to get home. Call it off-world insurance.

With two of the three components settled, all I needed was some dust to power it. Of course, I didn't have any dust. Even if there wasn't a shortage back home, I wasn't given time to get anything before Thera forced me through.

"Eirene, I need your help," I said to the jungle.

She appeared beside me.

"I've taken care of the demons. I need to borrow energy to open a portal to get rid of the bodies and equipment," I said.

She looked at Jarod sitting by the pile of gear. "You didn't get rid of them all."

"I need him to get your children back," I said. "I assumed that was the most important thing."

"When will my children return?"

"They should be back in . . . two kuu."

"Very well. You already have the power you need. Channel the energy into your circle when you're ready." She disappeared.

I knelt in front of the circle. I wasn't exactly sure how this was going to work. I'd just *heal* the circle? I held a hand out over it and let the energy flow. The circle began to glow with a deep blue light. I whispered the incantation and a portal opened. It started as a speck of light and grew to roughly eight feet in diameter. I could see the inside of the barn behind my house, the location I had been focusing on.

"Alright, move everything through," I said.

Jarod looked at the giant pile in front of us. "Are you going to help?"

"I have to keep the portal open," I said. "Hurry up."

I was hoping I could get a cell signal with the portal open. I hadn't looked at my phone since we left Earth. I pulled it out of my pocket to find it busted. It looked black and charred, as if it had short circuited or something. I guess the electricity Thera had hit me with had fried it. I tossed it through the portal with the growing pile of equipment. It took the three of them about thirty-five minutes to move the gear and bodies through and dump them into a big pile. They came back through the portal. Jarod picked up the last duffle bag of gear and tossed it through. I stopped channeling the energy and the portal slammed shut.

"What the hell?" Jarod shouted. "I thought we were going home?"

"We are but not yet," Mila said. "We have to get the animals back that your team took."

Jarod sighed. "Fine. Do your little magic trick and let's get it done."

I shook my head. "I can't do that. I've never been to the place before. You have to concentrate on the place you want to go. I can get us close, but you said they open the portal from where the animals are kept. So we wait for them."

The area had been quiet since the animals fled the humans, but now they started to return. The jungle slowly but surely came alive around us. I was confident by this time tomorrow everything would be back to normal for Eirene. I didn't *think* the animals would pose any threat to us at this point, but I was grateful for the goroo oil and the cleared trees supplying us with a buffer.

Most of the time the work I do seems temporary. Yes, I may stop some evil and save some lives but there's always something around the corner to start over with. I looked forward to the day humans got some sense and demons lost interest in our world, not that I believed I'd still be around to see it.

Jarod had been stewing in the now vacant campsite for close to twenty minutes before he spoke. "Why haven't you killed me already? What are you waiting for?"

Mila chuckled. "He's so dramatic."

"How long until your people open the portal?" I asked.

"That's it then? You'll kill me when the portal opens?"

I sighed. "If I intended to kill you, I'd have done it already. How long?"

Jarod fidgeted uncomfortably and looked at his watch. "If they're on schedule, six minutes."

"Here's what's gonna happen. When the portal opens, you're gonna go through in front of me. Mila and I are gonna kill everybody there, except for you, and send the missing animals back through. If we get separated, make your way southeast to Morrison Salvage in Dawsonville. Tell them that Obie sent you and they will keep you safe until I get there. Then I'll take you home."

"Can't I just take a bus?" Jarod asked.

"You can do whatever you want," Mila said. "Out of those choices, listening is probably the smartest."

I stood and shook out my arms and legs. "After I get the animals back, I'm getting a team together and clearing the house. Until I take those bastards out you need to stay out of sight. I don't want you getting caught in the middle."

"Alright, fair enough," Jarod said.

"How long?"

Jarod looked at his watch. "Two minutes."

The portal opened exactly on time. I took Jarod by the back of his collar and as soon as the portal was large enough pushed him through in front of me with Mila right on our tail. We came out into a barn with a number of stalls and cages. The man who had opened the portal stood in front of us. I pushed Jarod to the side and with a single strike cut the man down. With the portal's power severed it slammed shut behind us. There were two other men in the barn. They were wholly unprepared for an attack.

One man ran for the door. I was on him in an instant. I slammed into him, the momentum of my charge sandwiching him between a beam and my body. He let out a wheeze as the air was pushed from his lungs. I bit into his neck. Blood poured into my mouth. Struggling to breathe, he began to gurgle while blood filled his lungs. I threw him to the ground. The other man stuck a long cattle prod into my belly and pulled the trigger. Pain exploded through my abdomen. I grabbed the rod and pulled it out of my stomach. The man let go and turned to run out a side door. I threw my blade at his back.

I'd like to tell you it spun through the air and embedded itself deep between his shoulders, but the truth is, I was still new to blade throwing. It spun and it hit him, but didn't stick. He screamed and fell. The blade bounced off to the left. Blood soaked through his shirt. He started to get up. I pinned him to the ground with a foot on his back. He squirmed from the pain of having my paw pressed into his fresh wound. I gave his head a couple stomps. He didn't move anymore.

I rubbed the still tingling spot on my belly where the cattle prod had got me. "You couldn't have helped?" I said to Mila.

"There were only two." She shrugged. "You had it handled."

I suddenly felt a nauseous anxiety, the feeling I got when someone touched my blade. I turned to see Jarod had picked it up.

"We still have a deal, right?" he asked. "You won't kill me?"

"We have a deal but pulling a weapon on me is breach of contract."

Looking uncertain he turned the weapon around to hold it by the blade. He held the handle out to me. I exhaled a heavy breath as the uneasy feeling subsided. I put the blade back in its sheath and gave the barn a quick once over. The cages looked to be about half full with an assortment of Eirene's children. I didn't recognize any of them. It occurred to me I hadn't actually seen much wildlife during my stay with Eirene.

I found the keys on the body of the man that had opened the portal. "Is this doctor Tsukimora?"

"No," Jarod said. "That's Dean, or was Dean, I guess. Doctor Tsukimora rarely leaves the house."

"I'm going to make sure no one's coming."

I peeked out the main door at the house. It was definitely the same house Mila and I had been looking at when I was forced though the portal. I saw a figure on the front porch. I thought I was seeing things are first. It was Torch. Hank's youngest son was standing on the porch by the front door, appearing to be standing guard. He was wearing jeans and a tee shirt with his Tortured Occult kutte.

I motioned Jarod over. "What do you know about that guy?"

"Nothing much," Jarod said. "He's a machine. Never smiles and is always working. I don't think he sleeps."

"Start opening the cages," I said, tossing the keys to Jarod. "Thera, I have Eirene's children. They're ready to go back."

Thera appeared on the far side of the barn. A portal opened beside her with Eirene standing on the other side. We began to shepherd the animals out of the pens and through the portal. They were hesitant at first but as soon as they saw their home world they moved with a purpose.

"Some are missing," Eirene said from the other side of the portal.

"They aren't here. I'll keep looking," I said.

Thera disappeared and the portal closed.

"Who were you talking to?" Jarod asked.

"Don't worry about it," I said. "Listen, I appreciate your help. You've held up your end of the deal and I'll hold up mine. I need to check something. Go with Mila, I'll catch up."

"Hopefully, my car's still close by," Mila said.

If I hadn't spotted Torch, I would call this a job well done and move on to hunting down Holt and doctor Tsukimora. Yes, there were some missing animals, but if they weren't in the pens, they were most likely already victims of whatever they were brought here for. We would find answers in the house.

Hank had been looking for Torch for months. If I had a chance to bring him home, I had to take it. Still, it didn't look as if he was a prisoner. There were a lot of unanswered questions, lucky for me the person with all the answers was in front of me. I slid the door open a little more to get a view of the area. It looked clear but the people I killed would be missed soon. I had a short window to act before the alarm was raised. I moved across the yard. Torch saw me coming and took a few steps toward me. He had a blank expression. I didn't see any indication that he recognized me.

"Torch, we've been looking for you everywhere," I said. "We gotta go."

Torch jumped off the porch. I could feel the shockwave run through the earth when he landed. His feet sank into the earth a couple inches. The ground wasn't particularly soft, so the only conclusion was that he was heavy . . . *too* heavy. He lunged for me. I avoided him. He was slower than normal; we'd sparred many times over the years so I knew his moves. He threw punches. I maneuvered, easily avoiding his strikes.

"Snap out of it," I said. "Something's happened to you. Let me help."

I ducked a punch that contacted the railing of the porch steps. The railing ripped off the stairs. Everyone in the house must have heard it. A few figures appeared in the windows. Torch took advantage of my momentary distraction. He grabbed me by the throat, lifting me off the ground. I tried to pry his hand open but I couldn't budge it. It didn't feel normal. It was cold and there wasn't any of the normal give of flesh to it.

I punched a pressure point behind his elbow. It felt like I was punching stone. Pain shot through my hand. He started squeezing my throat. I grabbed my blade from its sheath and stabbed him in the chest. The blade barely bit in and there wasn't any blood. I began to gag from the pressure. I had to get loose soon or I wouldn't get free at all. I started to panic. I brought the blade down on his head, chest, and shoulders. It cut through his clothes but didn't seem to hurt him at all. My vision started to go dark around the edges. I was suddenly free, landing awkwardly on my back.

I looked up to see a severed arm flopping down the bank to the river. Torch began to disintegrate in front of me, crumbling into a pile of earth. I got to my knees gasping for breath. Three dark figures came around the side of the house. They weren't human. They looked like large cats, tigers or panthers, made of tar. They sort of oozed as they moved. These must have been what took Holt. I had no intention of letting them get me too. I grabbed Torch's kutte out of the dirt and ran for the river. The tar monsters charged after me. I dove into the water, disappearing under the surface.

CHAPTER • 21

I surfaced. The tar cats prowled back and forth along the water's edge. It didn't look as if they would come in and that was fine with me. I sheathed my blade and put on Torch's kutte to free my hands to swim. Upriver, the old bridge was three hundred yards away. I could try to flag down a car. I'd have to figure out how to lose the tar cats before I could get out of the water. Downstream, the water poured over the dam that ran parallel to the house. Below that the river disappeared into the woods.

Footsteps and shouting from the house told me I was out of time to decide. Two men with rifles ran out onto the top floor balcony. I dove underwater and swam downstream. The two men opened fire. The water was only five or six feet deep but it was enough to protect me from the bullets. Their supersonic rounds broke up on contact with the water, only penetrating a few inches. I jumped over the dam and pressed my back against the natural stone wall. The water pouring over the dam left me with enough room to keep my head out of the water between the wall and the wave.

Dark figures moved on the bank. I was out manned here, I'd need to get some backup. I didn't know if they knew where I was. If not, I didn't want to give my position away. I took a deep breath and slid into the water below the wave. This didn't go as smoothly as I'd hoped. The water churned there in a circle pulling everything back toward the damn. After getting tossed around in it I was able to swim down below the current and escape.

I could hold my breath for close to ten minutes. I swam, weaving my way through the rocks lining the river bottom. When I felt the need for air, I came up slowly, just sticking my nose out of the water. I took a few breaths, inhaled deeply, and slipped under the surface leaving barely a ripple on the surface.

I swam as far as I could for another breath. When my air gave out, I stuck my head out of the water for a look around. All I heard was the flow of the water and the rhythmic chirp of cicadas. It looked clear but I wasn't ready to get out of the water just yet. It occurred to me Mila's friend Jessie lived just off the river. I could keep swimming downstream until I found the house. Maybe I could lay low there until Mila could get me. Hopefully she and Jarod had gotten away.

I swam several miles before I saw lights off the house in the distance. I came up behind the house through the woods. The flicker of a television came through the windows. I crept up slowly, pausing every so often to listen for the tar monsters. Peeking in, I saw Jessie on a sofa, wrapped in a blanket, eating popcorn. In her human form, she was young and thin with blonde hair. Oreo lay on the couch beside her. The little dog lifted its head and started barking in my direction. I ducked to avoid being seen. I needed her help and being caught peeking in her windows wasn't the way to get it.

I went around to the front of the house. If I were lucky Mila would have stopped here first. A blue sedan was in the carport, but no sign of Mila. I absent mindedly reached for my phone only to remember it wasn't in my pocket. Oreo was still losing her mind inside the house.

Jessie would be looking out any second to see what was responsible for the ruckus.

As if on cue the door opened and Oreo came bounding out, barking viciously. If she was a bigger dog I might have been worried, as it was, she wasn't a threat.

Jessie looked annoyed. "You couldn't have called ahead?"

"I really couldn't."

"Well, I haven't looked into the address yet. I've been busy." Jessie crossed her arms and cocked her head to one side. "I told you I'd call when I had something."

Oreo added growling into the barking. The incessant yapping of little dogs always annoyed me. Why can't they just accept that a small stature isn't a reflection on their worth as dogs?

"I need to make a call. Can I come in?"

Jessie scoffed. "And drip all over the carpet?"

That's when I realized, Oreo wasn't barking at me anymore. Something in the woods had her attention. It was too dark for me to see what she was barking at. I sniffed the air and caught the chemical scent I had smelled in Eddie's trailer. I took a step into the house bumping into Jessie.

"Hey!" she shouted, trying to shove me out the door.

A tar cat came out from around the edge of the carport.

It lowered its head and made a low-pitched whistling sound. I could see air pushing through the tar on its back. The same sound came from somewhere off in the woods to my left. It went quiet and prowled into the yard toward us. I put my hand on my blade but didn't draw it. I didn't think it would be an effective weapon in this situation. This cat was more liquid than solid, so cutting it probably wouldn't do much damage, and from what I've seen, they engulfed their victims. Close combat was a losing proposition.

Jessie gasped when she spotted the thing from the doorway. "Oreo, get back inside!"

Oreo ignored her. Barking wildly, she charged the tar monster and took the cat's attention away from me. Leaves crunched behind me; a second cat was on its way. The first cat lunged at Oreo. The little dog leapt back to avoid it. I charged into the house, picking up Jessie, and slammed the door.

She screamed in my ear loud enough to make it start ringing. She hit me. I tossed her on the floor of the hallway.

"Got a setta pipes on you, don't you?" I asked, rubbing my ear. "Where are your car keys?"

"Go get my dog!" she screamed.

"You need to worry about how we're gonna get outta here more than what's going on outside."

The barking stopped.

"Keys!" I shouted.

Jessie got to her feet. "Right there," she said, pointing to a table by the front door.

I spotted a keychain clump about the size of a baseball. I grabbed it just as a tar cat slammed against the door, splattering tar across the window. I took a step back, glad to see the structural integrity of the door was holding . . . for now.

"What are those things?" Jessie asked.

"Trouble. We need to get outta here now."

The tar on the window flowed out of sight. There was a second collision. The impact ripped the bottom hinge from the wall, leaving a crack between the door and the frame. While it would have still blocked the entry of a more solid being, the tar began to flow in around the door.

"Let's go," I said, pushing Jessie down the hall. "Do you have a back door?"

"This way!"

The back door had a large window in the middle that gave a clear view of the yard outside. I ran into Jessie when she suddenly stopped.

"There's another one out there," she said.

We ran back into the hallway. A large puddle of tar was starting to take shape by the front door. I ran into the living room, looking for a way out. I grabbed a recliner and tossed it through the double windows on the back wall. I jumped out the window, landed on the recliner, and toppled over. I looked up to see if Jessie was going to follow me. She appeared in the window with a phone in her hand.

I held a hand out for her. "We gotta go!"

She put a foot on the window ledge and the hand with the phone in mine. Black sludge exploded over her and the window. I jerked my hand back, bringing the phone with it. Our eyes met, I could see the fear and silent pleading for help on her face. She grabbed the window sill, struggling to pull herself free from the tar. I reached to pull her free, but stopped short when the tar covered her face. It gave her another tug and she disappeared into the house.

"Sorry, Jessie," I said.

I ran for the carport, flipping through an unnecessary amount of flair on the keychain until I found the key I was looking for. I jumped into the sedan, tossed the phone into the passenger seat, and cranked the engine. I didn't see any movement in the house when I headed down the driveway. I would figure out how to get to the interstate after I put some distance between me and these monsters. I watched the house in the rearview. I was sure the two back there wouldn't be able to catch up to me. They were quick, sure, but not interstate speeds.

The third tar cat appeared in the road in front of me. It charged toward the car. If it wanted a game of chicken that was alright with me. I hit the gas. The monster never turned away. It collided with the front of the car and splattered. I turned on the wipers and hit the fluid to clear what had made it into the windshield. I changed into my human form as the smell of burning tar filled the car. I rolled down the window for some fresh air and checked the gas. Half a tank, enough to get me home.

CHAPTER · 22

The car was trashed, and not because I had run over a tar cat with it. The floorboards were full of fast food wrappers, mail that had been opened, some that hadn't, and other assorted trash. The cupholders were packed with makeup, bobby pins, hair ties, lighters, and more smaller bits of trash.

"By the Mother, Jessie's a slob," I said.

It was hard to see through the windshield with tar splattered all over it. The wipers hadn't done much more than smear it around the glass. I kept at it with the wipers until the fluid ran dry. By the time I made it to the interstate there was little more than hazy streaks. It wasn't ideal but it was good enough to get me home. The headlights on the car were dim, no doubt covered with sludge. I looked in the rearview mirror. There were plenty of cars behind me but none seemed to be following me. I took a deep breath, confident I'd made my escape.

I grabbed the phone from the passenger seat and dialed the only number I had memorized.

I recognized Tico's nonchalant, "Yep," when he answered.

"Tico, it's Obie. I need to talk to Hank."

His voice was muffled as if he were holding the phone below his chin. "He's busy. I'll have him call you when I see him."

"Alright," I said, fishing a pen out of the debris in the cupholder. "I need to talk to Hob, can you give me the number for the Southern Outpost?"

Tico let out a heavy sigh. "Don't you have it already?"

"I did, but not anymore so I need it."

"Hang on," he said.

I waited, listening to the sounds of clinking glasses and murmuring conversation. Tico came back on and rattled off ten digits that I scribbled onto my hand. I tossed the pen over my shoulder into the back seat and dialed the number on my hand.

I waited impatiently as it rang. A woman answered after the second ring. "Hey, Obie, It's Meghan. What can I do for you?"

After our little excursion into the demon world and Harlan's fall she had been put in charge of the Southern Outpost. I was happy about it. Since I'm the one who brought her back from the demon world, we got along like peaches and cream and that meant everyone at the outpost treated me with a modicum of respect.

"Hey, Meg, I need to talk to Hob. It's kind of urgent."

"Okay, hang on."

The line went silent. Since Hob worked with Queen Isabelle getting in touch with him meant jumping through hoops.

Finally, I was routed to Hob. "*Ja, hello.*"

I put the phone on speaker and placed it on the dash. "Hey, Hob, sorry to bug you. I wanted to ask you about some magic I ran into."

"*Gute Nacht,* Obie, there is no bugging me. It is good to hear from you," Hob said. "Tell me about this magic."

"It was a man made out of dirt, well . . . mostly dirt. As far as I could tell it was a real arm on a dirt body."

"*Ja,* it sounds like the golem," Hob said.

"What, that guy from *Lord of the Rings?*"

There was a moment of silence before Hob answered. "*Nein,* the golem is made of earth. Let me ask you, Obie, did the creature speak?"

"No, I don't think it could. I tried talking to it, but it didn't say anything back."

"You say it had an arm from a living person?" Hob asked. "Was there a paper in its mouth?"

"It kept its mouth closed, so I don't know about the paper, but I hit it with my blade a few times. It didn't do anything until I severed the arm, then the body fell apart into a pile of dirt."

"A golem is a formidable creature. They are a *Jüdish* creation *und* very strong," Hob said. "It is pure magic. The golem you speak of, however, uses a piece of a real person as the base ingredient. It is sloppy magic."

"So, the mage that did it is an amateur?" I asked.

"Oh, *Nein,* do not make the mistake of thinking this is unskilled," Hob said. "Whoever did this is powerful if not a little lazy perhaps."

That's when I noticed I could see through the windshield a little better. I'd given up on the wipers when the fluid ran out, so I couldn't think of any reason the windshield would have cleared. The headlights seemed brighter as well. I sped up to get beside a car and compared how bright the headlights were. No question, the tar had definitely cleared. It's possible the tar dripped off. Who knows what happened to those things when they were killed. Then again, if it wasn't dead . . .

"Obie? Have I lost you?"

"Hob, I'll have to call you back." I rolled up the window.

If that thing was still alive I didn't want to be stuck in a confined space when it had congealed enough to come after me. Even if it didn't attack me in the car, I couldn't risk taking it back to the clubhouse. If we didn't manage to eliminate the facility, I didn't want to let them know about the T.O.

"Shit," I said. "What do I do now?"

"Everything alright?" Hob asked.

Apparently he hadn't hung up.

"Yep, talk soon," I said and hung up.

I held my feet off the floor while picturing tar pouring from under the dash. Before I knew it, I'd be up to my knees and that would be it for me. I'd get hauled off to that facility never to be heard from again. It was hard to keep the gas pressed while holding my feet off the floor. The car began to lurch.

Sludge oozed from the vents and ran down the dashboard. I unbuckled the seatbelt and crouched on the driver's seat. The car coasted down from eighty miles per hour. I was going to have to jump. I reached for a lighter from the cup holder. I ended up with a gum wrapper and a zip tie as well. I put the zip tie in my mouth and grabbed some of the mail from the passenger seat. I lit the paper with the lighter. Flame licked my fingers.

I held the flame to the tar. It began to burn and retreated into the vents. I tossed the burning paper into the floorboard and reached for more. I lit everything I could find that would burn and tossed it around the car. The cab began to fill with smoke, not just smoke from burning paper, but harsh chemical smoke that burned thick and black and hurt my lungs.

Fire burst from the vents. Tar poured out and ran down the dash. It seemed to move by a force other than gravity telling me it wasn't dead, at least not yet. That left me without any real options. Getting swallowed by one of these things would be bad enough, with it on fire . . . let's just say a lava bath wasn't on my to-do list.

I waved a hand in front of the speedometer to clear the smoke enough to get an idea how fast I was going. I'd coasted down to fifty-five. The smoke burned my lungs. I coughed. I looked in the rearview mirror and didn't see any headlights directly behind me. It was going to be bad enough to jump out of a moving car, I didn't want to get run over in the process. I opened the door and rolled out.

I woke up, aching all over, lying against the barrier at the center of the interstate. A man stood over me. He wore work boots, jeans, and a tee shirt. I had an excellent view of the boots. They had traces of paint, different colors in irregular patterns, clearly a painter by trade. A baseball cap was pushed far back on his head. He scratched his forehead with one hand and held a phone to his ear with the other.

"It's real bad," he said. "A bunch of the lanes are blocked, one car's on fire."

I groaned, pulling myself into a sitting position and realized the zip tie was still in my mouth. I leaned against the concrete barrier, pulling the zip tie out, and looked at it. There were teeth marks in the plastic. I shoved it in my pocket.

The man knelt in front of me. "Jesus, I thought you were dead."

"Not yet," I grunted. "Help me up."

"I really think you should stay put. There's an ambulance on the way."

"I'm getting up with or without you."

The man looked around nervously before taking my hand. "Just take it easy, okay?"

"Don't worry about me. I'll be fine." I got to my feet.

As I tried to stretch out the aches I could see the burning car sixty feet ahead. I couldn't tell how many cars were involved in the pile up. I thought the car would coast off the road and come to a stop. I guess that didn't work out as planned. It looked like the far left lane was still open and some cars were moving around the wreck on the right shoulder.

I'd need to find a car to make it back to the clubhouse. I'd walk to the next off ramp, find a car to rent or *borrow,* and get back on the road. The cars around me were moving at a snail's pace so getting to the other side wouldn't be a problem. I limped into traffic, giving the cars I walked in front of a courteous wave as I went. I could see the lights of emergency vehicles working their way though the traffic. Two lanes over I used the hood of an old pickup to brace myself. I raised my hand in an apologetic wave and stopped in my tracks when I saw the driver. It was Jarod. I limped over to the passenger seat, opened the door, and eased in.

"Uh . . . This isn't the ambulance buddy." Jarod said.

I put my head back and closed my eyes. "Yeah, I need a ride and we're going to the same place. It's me, Obie."

CHAPTER · 23

"It was just a big charred spot with some melted plastic and broken glass," Jarod said. "It burned hot, too. The branches above where the car was parked were wilted."

"How did Mila take her car getting burned up?" I asked.

"She just stared for a few minutes and then we left. She, uh, *found* this truck for me and told me to head to Morrison Salvage. She said she had to find the guy that did it. I'm glad I'm not him. He's going to get it."

I shook my head. "Nah. She won't hurt him, she's helping him."

"Why would she help someone who lit her car on fire?"

I sighed. "Its complicated. We're Keepers, it's what we do."

"I saw how you helped the guys at the camp," Jarod mumbled under his breath.

He probably thought I couldn't hear it, and if I was human I wouldn't have. "Sometimes helping people means hurting other people. I don't like it but that's the way it is."

We drove the rest of the ride in silence. I was feeling a little paranoid after my adventure in the car so the first thing I did when we got to the clubhouse was check the truck for traces of tar. I didn't see any. I crammed Torch's kutte into the pocket of my cargo shorts. It stuck out of the top a bit but it was good enough.

"You're about to see a world you've never seen before," I said, walking with Jarod to the clubhouse. "You've dealt with people like this before but you didn't know it. They like to stay outta sight. Most of the folks in here can hear very well, so just keep your mouth shut and you'll be fine."

I shifted to krasis in the changing room and took Jarod into the bar. As soon as we entered he stopped in his tracks. His eyes grew wide. Trolls, goblins, orcs, not to mention a number of shifters filled the room.

I took him by the arm and pulled him toward the bar. "Be cool," I whispered.

I waved Tico over.

Tico gave the air a couple sniffs. "Human?"

"This is Jarod," I said. "He'll be hanging out here for a while. Put him on my tab."

"Humpf," Tico scoffed. "What can I get ya?"

"You have Johnny Walker?" Jarod asked.

"How's blue label sound?" Tico asked.

Jarod shrugged. "I mean . . . yeah, if Obie's good with it."

I leaned an elbow against the bar. "Why wouldn't I be good with it?"

"It's about fifty dollars a shot," Jarod said.

"Fifty-five," Tico corrected. "That's nothin' for a big shot like you right?"

"Sure, whatever," I said.

Tico went to get Jarod's drink.

"He's kind of a douche but he's a good bartender," I said.

"So, you want me to hang out at a bar full of . . . Whatever these folks are, and drink for free?" he asked.

"That sums it up," I said.

"Cool."

Tico placed a glass on the table in front of Jarod. "Obie, why are you such an ass?"

Jarod picked up the glass. "They do have good hearing," he mumbled.

I flashed Tico an insincere smile. "Where's Hank?"

"Conference room," Tico said motioning with his head.

I walked around the bar toward the back hallway.

"Listen, don't worry about the cost of drinks," Tico said. "Obie has more money than God. Did you know he's footing the bill to send his ex traveling all over the world on an indefinite trip? She's probably out banging her way across the country right now. The point is, we're going to have some fun on Obie's dime. I've got some Lewis XIII cognac you need to try next."

I opened the door to the back and looked back at the bar. Tico gave me the same smile I'd given him a moment before.

I sighed. I gave Cotton a nod in the kitchen and went to the conference room. I knocked on the door as I opened it. Hank was sitting at the table, looking through a stack of papers.

"Have a second?"

"Yeah, just club business." He put the paper in his hand down on the stack. "I'm glad to have a break honestly."

The most important thing I needed to talk to him about was Torch but I wasn't sure how to broach that subject so I started off with something a little lighter. "How's Doc Lin's husband?"

"William . . . He's still alive if that's what you're asking," Hank said. "And he's still locked up. If it weren't for Doc we would've had this wrapped up already. Given him a beating, convinced him to stay away . . . Doc's been a good friend to the club but I can't have him comin' around causing trouble."

"If you are sure he won't talk or come back causing trouble you'll let him go?"

Hank shifted in his seat. "It's not that simple. We have rules. Folks don't get to come to our house with a gun and just walk away. I want this whole fucking mess to go away. It gives me a headache."

"And if the club had more important things to worry about?" I asked. "William apologizes and slips out the back?"

Hank's expression hardened. "What aren't you telling me?

I pulled Torch's kutte from my pocket and draped it on the table in front of him.

His voice took an urgent tone. "Where'd you get this from?"

"Is it Torch's?" I asked. "It's not a knockoff or something?"

Hank took the kutte and looked it over closely inside and out, sticking his fingers through the cuts I had made with my blade. "It's Torch's . . . I'm sure. After so long I knew he was probably dead. I'd hoped to find him alive, but I think I knew deep down I was fooling myself."

"We don't know he's dead, not for sure."

"If he wasn't dead he'd still be wearing this," he said. "Where'd you get it."

"I'd tracked Holt to an old house a couple hours northwest of here. I was about to go in and get him when Thera shows up and sent me on a job. When I get back I see what I thought was Torch standing in front of this house. I tried to talk to him but he attacked me. Turns out it wasn't him at all. I talked to Hob about it and he thinks it was a golem. When I got away from it, it collapsed into a pile of dirt. I grabbed the kutte and made a run for it. I almost didn't get away. There were armed guards that started shooting as well as the same tar things that took Holt. Besides the kutte, I have someone that spotted him alive and well two weeks ago."

"Who?"

"A wolf named Atticus," I said. "He says Torch told him to find me. He's the one that led us to the facility."

"I want to talk to him," Hank said. "Where is he?"

"Heh heh, well . . . We lost him." I scratched the back of my neck.

"But Mila's tracking him down right now. I'm not waiting on her though. I'm heading to the facility and I'm getting them both back."

Hank leaned forward. "Do I need to tell you the T.O.'s coming along on this?"

"And here I was gonna ask you for help." I chuckled.

"Do you have a plan?"

"The house is a fortress. I think I saw a back entrance on the river. They won't expect an attack from there. I'll go in the back and we'll meet in the middle."

"I'll get the club together," Hank said. "We'll be ready in about an hour."

"And the William situation?" I asked.

"Get him to apologize and he can go."

CHAPTER • 24

There wasn't a guard in front of William's room. Even if he got out some-how, he couldn't get out of the building. Without a silver weapon he posed absolutely no threat to the T.O. beyond being able to reveal what they were. The key to the deadbolt hung on a nail in the doorframe. I changed to my human form, used the key, and went inside. William lay on the bed with his eyes buried in the crook of his elbow. The room was plain with just the bed, a small desk, and a chair.

Will looked out from under his elbow. He sat up, sitting on the edge of the bed. "Well?"

"I'm Obie."

"You can't keep me here," he said. "Eventually someone will figure out where I am and come looking for me."

I pulled a chair from the desk in the corner, placed it in front of the bed, and sat down. "Will, you seem like a smart guy. I'm surprised you ha-ven't figured out that that's not a good thing for you." He didn't respond so I continued. "I don't think you understand what kind of trouble you're in. I know you don't understand the trouble you made for Rebecca. I am going to do my best to be truthful with you. I'll answer any questions you have, if I can."

He turned his head to the side and squinted at me. "How do you know my wife?"

"About three years ago Rebecca was in a car wreck. Collision at a red light," I said. "You remember that?"

Will nodded. "The drunk driver? It was a miracle she wasn't killed. The car was totaled, cops never found the guy."

"It wasn't a miracle." I sighed. "I was chasing someone. They drove their car through the light and plowed into the side of her car. They ran off. I probably could have caught him right there, but I checked on the car he hit rather than chase him. I try to prevent collateral damage like that if I can. Some in my line of work don't bother but I think it's the right thing to do. Anyway, I found Rebecca in bad shape. I healed her."

"What do you mean you *healed* her?" he asked.

"You've heard of laying on hands? Faith healing?" I asked. "That's the closest thing to what I do. She woke up, almost good as new."

"Yeah, you really think I'm going to believe that?"

"She wouldn't have believed it either if she hadn't seen it," I said. "You said yourself it was a miracle."

I could see him thinking, wondering if what I was telling him could be true. "That's bullshit."

I shot him a smile. "We'll see."

"So what is this like Stockholm Syndrome or something?" he asked.

"I already told you, It's not like that."

He leaned forward, putting his elbows on his knees and wrung his hands. "Then how do you explain the lying and late nights? Disappearing at all hours, saying there's an emergency at the hospital? I went by the hospital and they told me she hadn't worked there in over a month."

"I don't know what she was telling you. It never occurred to me, to be honest, but she's still practicing medicine, just in a different way."

"Then explain to me what's so special about this place that she leaves her job as chief of medicine to work in a biker bar."

"I can't tell you that," I said.

Will smirked. "You can but you won't."

"That's fair," I said, "but it doesn't change anything. We both want the same thing, to get you outta here."

"I don't even know why they're keeping me," Will said. "I'd understand if they beat me up and tossed me out or something but kidnapping?"

"Rebecca's been a big help around here and they don't want to damage that relationship by damaging you. At the same time, coming here with a gun causing trouble requires a response. No one does that and leaves untouched." I leaned back in the chair. "You happened to come here at the worst time. There's a lot going on which is going to work in your favor. You need to apologize for intruding and make Hank believe you won't cause anymore trouble. Do that and you walk away."

Will sneered. "Yeah, that's going to be a no from me."

"What's the hold up here, Will? You can't enjoy being here."

He looked me straight in the eye. "It's that I don't believe a word you're saying."

"Okay, I guess a demonstration is in order." I stood and turned, showing him my back flattening my tee shirt against my skin. "Nothing here right?"

I turned back, putting my arm behind me so he couldn't see it, took a deep breath, and focused on changing my blade hand to krasis. I didn't want to make a full change; Will didn't need that much convincing. When I could feel the claws on my fingertips I reached into krasis on my back and pulled out my blade. I changed my hand back to its human orientation. His eyes went wide as the two-foot blade appeared seemingly out of nowhere.

"Do you believe this is real?" I asked, holding the blade out for him to inspect.

He reached forward hesitantly and gave it a little pinch. "Yes."

I sat and lined the tip of the blade up with my forearm. I gritted my teeth and with a quick thrust I put it all the way through. I let go of the handle and held the impaled arm out to him. Blood ran from the injury, dripping on the floor.

I held the arm out to him. "Is this real, Will? Do I have a piece of metal going though my arm?"

He had slid back on the bed against the wall and didn't look like he wanted to give it a close inspection.

I stood and took a step toward him. "Don't be shy, Will, its not like anyone's bleeding to death here."

He held his hands up and looked away. "Fine, yes . . . I believe you!"

"Alright," I said, sitting back down. "Pay attention now, this is where it gets good."

He cringed when I pulled the blade free and stuck it into the floor. I held a hand over the injury and began channeling energy. My eyes and hands emitted a blue aura and I gave my hand a little shake for good measure. It's not that I could heal myself any faster than I already did but I could put on a little show.

When the injury had closed, I wiped the blood from my arm on my pants and held it out to him. He slid forward for a better look.

"So, you can believe what you've seen and that I'm telling you the truth. That I saved Rebecca's life, that she is working in medicine here, and that anything you aren't being told is for your safety. You can accept that I'm trying to help you and that the only way out of this is for you is to apologize. Or I can give you a more *personal* demonstration."

"What about all the lying?" he asked.

I shrugged. "That's between you and her."

"I'll apologize."

I headed out the door. "Don't touch that," I said, pointing to my blade. "I'll know if you do."

I found Hank in the bar talking to Mila.

"Will needs to talk to you," I told Hank.

"What's he gonna say?"

"I think he's ready to leave."

Hank nodded. "You coming?"

"I'll be right in."

Hank went to talk to Will, leaving me with Mila.

"Did you find Atticus?"

"Yeah," Mila said. "He's outside."

"Give me a sec to wrap this up and we'll ride together," I said.

I went back to see how things were going with Will and Hank.

Will had his head down in mid-sentence when I walked in. "...wrong of me to come here and I'm sorry for the trouble I've caused. If you're willing, I'd like to pretend this never happened. I won't say anything to anyone. I've been in bed with the flu for the past few days."

"Alright," Hank said. "I'll have Rebecca take you home. Don't come back."

CHAPTER • 25

"I don't see why I need this," I said. "I'm not even interested."

Mila gave me a pitying smile. "I don't know how you've stayed so innocent all this time. It's not 1875 anymore. Nowadays, people use apps."

Mila and I sat on my truck's tailgate, waiting for the Tortured Occult. I couldn't tell why she was so interested in finding me a date and I wasn't sure how I felt about using an app to do it. I hadn't told her I planned to track down Naylet. I was sure she would just tell me all the things wrong with my plan. Thera wouldn't let me run off; things might not go as I want with Naylet . . . I knew all that. I would just have to figure it out.

A rattling car passed in front of the gas station where we were parked. It looked to be patched together parts from many junkyard trips, leaving it with mismatched paint. A frankencar. I watched it disappear down the remote country road before looking back at the screen Mila held out to me.

"Alright, it's easy," Mila said. "A picture comes up and if you like what you see you put your finger on the screen and push the picture to the right. If you aren't interested then you push it to the left. Swipe right and swipe left, get it?"

I sighed. "What I'm not getting is, how could I know if I want to court any of these women from a picture and a few sentences?"

"By the Mother! *Court?* Do ya hear yourself? Who talks like that?"

"I haven't been single for a very long time." I raised an eyebrow with annoyance. "And I've heard you speak the same way."

"I quit saying court for anything outside of legal proceedings by 1950. Just touch their profile to get more info," she said. "We haven't finished your profile yet, so you haven't got that far."

The screen showed a young blonde woman with the user name Ashleigh. She had some pictures with a cat and some with friends. She had a couple paragraphs that didn't really tell me anything about her. Content without substance. I suddenly felt much more out of touch than I ever had before.

"This isn't really telling me much," I said. "How do I know if I want to swipe her?"

"You're overthinking it," Mila said. "This is less with your head and more with your . . . you know."

"Heart?"

Mila grinned. "Think a little lower."

"Gut?"

"Keep going. You'll get there eventually."

I heard the rumble of motorcycles in the distance. Mila turned the phone off and slid it into her pocket. The Tortured Occult rode up in two rows and pulled into the parking lot. They backed their motorcycles into a neat row and killed the engines. Hank, Big Ticket, and Cotton got off their bikes and joined us at the car.

I opened the back door of the truck. Atticus climbed out, his muzzle sticking out slightly from under his hoodie. I didn't really want to bring him but it was what it was.

"This the guy?" Hank asked.

"This is Atticus, he escaped the facility with Torch's help." I turned to Atticus. "Tell them what you told me."

"There's a tunnel that goes into the lower levels of the facility. It looks like a storm cellar in the middle of the woods. If you can get in there, follow the hallway and go down the stairs, it will take you to the cells. If they have Torch, you'll find him there."

"Atticus told me you can see the house from the cellar door," I said. "I did some research. A real estate site with some pictures. The facility used to be a grist mill in the 1800s. It's been converted to hydropower, so I was thinking I'll kill the power and then you can get in quick and get to the cells before they figure out what's going on. The generator is on the back of the house by the river. From the pictures it looks like I can swim up to the generator and take out the power for you. I'll get in and meet you at the cells." I pointed west. "The house is about three miles up the road. We can leave the bikes here and take a shortcut through the woods."

"Alright, let's get it done," Hank said. "Remember, we want to take some alive if we can manage it. If Torch isn't there, I want to know what happened to him."

"We can expect to find other hostages besides Torch and Holt," I said. "Eddy was taken a couple days ago, as well as Jessie last night. There's no telling how many hostages they could have or what they're doing to them."

The T.O. left some prospects behind to watch the bikes. We headed off through the woods as a group. When we got within sight of the house I turned north, leaving the group behind. I needed to come in from upriver. I made my way to the river's edge. I looked around before I made the change to krasis. I wasn't really worried about being spotted, the area was remote and I had the cover of night. I slid into the cool water and swam lazily downstream, I wanted to make sure they had time to find the hatch and get into position.

I stopped under the old bridge and held onto the stone. I could see shadows moving around inside the house and one person strolling around the exterior. I didn't see any weapons on him. That didn't mean a whole lot. He could be a golem. There's no telling how many of them could be on the property—not to mention the tar cats. They seemed to be used to catch people, a kind of mobile trap. Still, if they were ordered to kill, or decided to, they could suffocate someone without any trouble.

I took a breath and dove under water. I swam into an alcove in the house's foundation. I found a ladder mounted to the concrete and climbed up. Peeking over the edge, I saw a large generator in the corner. There was a door to my right with a ladder and some tools on the back wall. I put my ear against the door but didn't hear anything. I tried the handle. Locked. The door looked to be made of cast iron, probably original to the house. Getting in this way might be a problem.

I realized I hadn't thought through how to actually disable the generator. I didn't really know what I was looking at. It reminded me of an engine, except without all the engine parts I was used to seeing. It had an on and off switch, but I had something more permanent in mind. I found some conduit running from the generator into a fuse box mounted to the wall. I found some tools and took the cover off the circuit breaker, revealing the wiring and switches. I hit the off switch on the generator, flipped the main breaker off, and pulled switches from the box and tossed them into the river behind me.

I pulled six of them before I heard the door lock click. I moved to the wall beside the door and pulled my blade. A man swung the door open and stepped out. I plunged my blade into his side, pushing him toward the railing. He screamed. I sank the claws of my left hand into his back enough to get a grip. My new-found handle and the weapon buried in his body gave me holds to pick him up and throw him into the river. The momentum pulled him off the blade. He belly flopped into the water below.

I stepped through the door into a hallway. It looked like a normal house, carpeted floors, a nice paint job with artwork on the walls. Not what I was expecting, not that I really knew what to expect. I could see the beam of a flashlight waving around past the hallway. I followed the hall, passing a couple bedrooms and a bathroom, to a living room where a man was using a flashlight to look for something under the couch. I'd been moving quietly but my first step into the room made a floorboard release a long groaning squeak.

"Will you get the lights on already? I dropped my card, I thought it went under the couch but I don't see it," the man said.

I stuck my blade into his back before he had time to realize I wasn't who he thought I was. He grunted in surprise. I gave the blade a twist as I pulled it back. He collapsed with shallow erratic breaths that ended a moment later. He dropped a phone he had been using as a flashlight.

It came to rest with the light pointing up. It reflected off the walls, resulting in a dim lighting that would have been romantic in a nice restaurant with some flowers and candles. The fresh corpse bleeding into the carpet would have killed the vibe.

The card he had mentioned was on the floor beside the couch. If he'd looked a few feet to the side he would have easily found it. I picked it up and gave it a quick once over. It had his picture on the front and was attached to a retractable lanyard. I tossed it over my shoulder. With the power out, I didn't have to worry about key cards. There was a door on the far side of the room with a card scanner. I tried the handle, the door swung open revealing a flight of stairs with a different look than the house I had seen so far.

The passageway was cold concrete and steel. I moved down the stairs and peeked around the corner. Emergency lights mounted to the ceiling thirty feet apart spun in their housings, throwing red light up and down the hallway. The light wasn't enough to illuminate the corridor completely, leaving long shadows that shifted with the moving lights making the corridor seem to churn with life.

CHAPTER · 26

I caught movement in the distance and heard the steady *clack* of footsteps echoing through the corridor. I flattened myself against the wall and waited as they approached. Peeking around the corner, I saw two men with guns coming in my direction. When they reached the corner, I spun out and hit the closest one, my blade easily cutting through him. He fell to the floor with a surprised wheeze as his last breath left his body.

The second man grabbed his pistol and brought it to bear. I swung at his weapon hand. Our weapons collided as he fired. I cringed from the muzzle blast, my ears screaming in protest. I was stunned momentarily. I looked over to see the man holding his right hand against his body. The gun and a thumb lay on the floor beside him. He bent to retrieve the weapon.

I leapt for him. He fell face first to the ground with me on his back. I bit the back of his head, my teeth scraping across his skull, filling my mouth with flesh and hair. I'd scalped him. He writhed underneath me. I spit out his scalp, gagging on the hair. A loud percussive *thump* hit my ears followed a moment later by pain shooting through my abdomen. I knew the sensation, I'd been shot. The gun pointed at my guts just before it went off for a second time. He had managed to get hold of it with his left hand, pointing it at me from under his body.

The gun flashed with a *thump.* The bullet tore into me a few inches away from the first. I pinned his hand to the floor. He pulled the trigger for the third time. The bullet slammed into the wall beside my head, sending concrete shards into my face. Keeping him pinned, I bit at his face and neck, tearing off bits and pieces until he didn't have any fight left in him.

I rolled off him and propped myself against the wall. I needed a couple minutes to recover after taking two to the gut. I used a claw to get the hair that was stuck in between my teeth and spit it out onto the floor. When the pain receded to a dull ache I got to my feet and continued down the hallway.

I caught movement in the distance, a lot of movement. Large figures were headed in my direction. At first I thought I might be in trouble, but then I recognized the group as the Tortured Occult. Hank led the group. We met in front of stairs going down to another level.

"What happened to you?" Hank asked.

I looked down to see the blood, some mine some not, covering my fur and clothes. "Just another day at the office. Have any trouble?"

"Nothing we couldn't handle."

Hank looked past me. He looked more confused than alarmed. He put a hand to my chest and moved me out of the way. Torch, or more likely a Torch golem, came up behind me.

Hank walked over slowly. "Torch?"

This Torch was wearing jeans, a grey tee shirt, and a canvas jacket. He wasn't wearing a kutte, which wasn't surprising since I'd taken the real one back with me. Torch and Hank walked up to each other. Torch sucker punched him. Hank took a hard shot to the face and fell limply to the ground. Ginsu charged Torch, taking a shot to the gut. Ginsu fell, holding one hand where he'd been hit.

The T.O. tackled the golem, taking it to the ground buried under a pile of bikers. If this Torch was like the last one, part was from the real Torch. If I found what part of this abomination was original hardware, I could remove it and destroy the creature. I knew it wasn't the left arm.

I stepped over Hank to the churning pile of bikers. "Hold him down," I said, drawing my blade.

Ginsu grabbed my arm holding the weapon from behind. "Don't," was all he could get out before hacking up blood that he wiped away with his arm.

"Relax," I said. "It's not Torch."

The club pinned the golem, giving me time to find what the real piece was. I could smell the sourness of meat starting to turn. I sniffed the right arm first, then the left leg. As soon as I gave the right leg a sniff, I knew I had found it. I cut the pant leg away and felt for the connection point. My stomach turned as I ran my hand over the cold flesh I knew was Torch's leg. Just below the knee I found the transition from flesh to stone. I swung. My first strike hit high putting a notch into the creature. The second swing hit the mark and cut through, the blade biting into the floor. The T.O. fell forward onto a pile as the golem lost its shape and melted into earth. I pulled my blade free from the floor and stuck it back into its sheath.

Big Ticket picked himself up off the floor. He spit out a mouthful of dirt. "What the fuck was that?"

"A golem," I said. "Anybody hurt?"

"Here," Ginsu said from behind me.

He sat against the wall breathing heavily, with strings of blood and saliva dripping onto his shirt. I held a hand over his chest and let the energy flow. His breathing smoothed out immediately.

He wiped his mouth on his arm and got to his feet before I had finished. "I'm good, check Hank."

I looked over to see Hank still lying face down on the floor. I knelt and flipped him over. A trickle of blood ran from his nose and ears. The club gathered around.

"He gonna be alright?" Lug Nut asked.

I put a hand on either side of his head to heal him. I could feel the energy flowing into him. "Yeah, he'll be fine."

After half a minute Hank came to. Cotton and Big Ticket each took and arm and pulled him to his feet.

"What happened?" Hank asked.

"A golem sucker punched you," Cotton said. "I thought we lost you."

Hank walked over to the pile of dirt and looked down at the leg. The dark skin had taken on a gray tint.

Hank nudged it with his foot. "What's this?"

"Hob said to make this type of golem it uses a body part from the person the golem is imitating," I said.

"Why didn't you tell me that earlier?" he asked.

"I didn't want you to lose hope that we'd find him alive."

Hank ran his tongue over his teeth. "You said you fought a golem of Torch earlier . . . What part did they use for it?"

"Left arm."

Hank nodded and turned to the club. "We're gonna kill every one of the motherfuckers. No mercy, rip 'em to pieces." He whispered in my ear, "You should have told me."

CHAPTER · 27

The revelation that someone here had been cutting Torch into pieces sent the Tortured Occult into a rage. They abandoned me and caution, rushing through the hallways like a wave, crashing over anyone they came into contact with. I was left behind listening to the erratic growls, screams, and gunfire echoing through the building.

I followed the T.O. at a more leisurely pace. The last place I wanted to be was in the middle of an enraged shifter mosh pit. Around the first corner I found the remains of some guards that looked like they had been dragged behind a truck. They'd been ripped apart to the point dental records might not be enough to identify them. Blood was splattered floor to ceiling with body parts and bits of flesh scattered down the hallway. There wasn't a way to move down the hallway without stepping in blood so I didn't try. I stepped over the worst of the mess making my way down the hallway.

A number of steel doors lined the hallway. Each door had a corresponding control panel full of levers, gauges, and buttons. At the end of the corridor was a pair of glass doors. The T.O. were piled up in front of the doors, pounding on them, trying to break them down. I couldn't see what had them so riled up.

I approached slowly. They would either break down the door and kill whoever was inside, or they would lose steam and calm down. Either one meant I didn't need to be in a hurry. I looked through a small window in the metal door. They were cells, the kind used for solitary confinement. Where you would expect to see at least a bed and a toilet, these were empty. They were concrete walls with drains in the floor. The most intricate part of the cell was the ceiling. It had recessed lighting with a number of pipes, conduit, and a sprinkler system all protected behind a heavy duty cage that ran wall to wall.

The muffled yapping of a small dog caught my attention. I followed the sound down two cells and looked inside. Jessie and Oreo were covered head to toe in tar. It took me a second to recognize them. I was glad to see they were safe . . . miserable from the looks of it, but safe. She saw me, got to her feet and came over to the window.

"Are you okay? I asked.

She gave me a death stare and the finger.

"I'll get you out, hang on."

I looked at the control panel beside the cell. I couldn't make much sense of it. There wasn't a clearly labeled *let your friends out* button. I tried hitting a button and flipped a switch. The door didn't open. I heard something from the cell; the sprinkler had come on. Jessie looked even more pissed. I decided it would be better to find someone who knew how to work the controls—if there were any still alive. The way the Tortured Occult was trying to break down the glass doors it was a safe bet there was someone in there.

I headed over to them. My curiosity got the better of me and I found myself pausing at each window to take a peek inside. In one cell, a woman huddled in the corner. The sprinkler system had a constant rain falling inside the cell. The woman looked damp and miserable. She shivered. I thought about turning off the sprinkler since it was the one control I knew how to operate. Then I thought of Atticus. He had been kept in a cell with the sprinklers on and was eager to get back. Could they have done the same thing to her as they did to him?

A person on the ground in the next cell made me do a doubletake. It was Torch. He sat propped up against the wall, missing an arm and both legs. I'd seen a golem made from an arm and a leg so far. There must be third running around somewhere. I knocked on the cell door to get his attention, but he didn't look up. Judging from the way Oreo's bark had been muffled the cells seemed to have some level of soundproofing. I gave the door three solid hits but he still didn't respond.

"Hank!" I shouted, moving from cell to cell, looking through the windows.

Most of the cells were empty; only a few had people in them. Besides Torch and the woman there was a werewolf sitting with his back to the door. There was no sign of Holt, maybe they had another cell block I hadn't seen yet? We hadn't searched the upstairs either. It's possible he could be held somewhere else on the property.

"Hank," I said again.

He was standing at the back of the ruckus watching the progress. Turning around he said, "There you are."

"Have you found Holt?"

"We haven't found anybody," he said. "Just clearing the facility."

I pointed to the cell with Torch. "We need someone alive to open these cells and tell me where they took Holt."

"There's three holed up in there," Fisheye said, emerging from the pack, wiping blood from his mouth to his arm. "Give me a blowtorch and I can get in there."

"We can't get in, but they can't get out either," I said. "We should secure the facility. That will give us time to get the gear we need and get some answers."

"Alright!" Hank shouted to the club. "Half of you get outside and keep watch. The rest of us will clear upstairs." He turned to Fisheye. "Call the prospects and have them bring up something to get that door open … and get the Tennessee chapter down here."

I pointed my chin in the direction of the door. "I'll watch them."

The Tortured Occult split up for their assignments. I approached the doors the T.O. had been trying to break down. It looked like plain sliding glass doors. The kind you would see at any supermarket. I could tell there was more to them from the pounding the club had given them. The glass was scratched all over with so much blood and spit smeared over them that it was hard to see inside. Using the heel of my hand I wiped a circle large enough to look through. There were three people inside, standing against the back wall. They were wearing scrubs, standing in what looked like an operating room any hospital would be proud to have.

The tallest woman walked over to a phone on the wall, picked it up, and dialed a few buttons. Her voice was muffled enough that I couldn't make out what she said. She hung up and went back to her place behind the table.

I took my blade and tried to stick it between the doors to pry them open. It didn't work. They seemed to have some kind of locking mechanism that kept them firmly in place. I thought about trying to break in but if the T.O. couldn't break it down it would probably take me a week to chop a hole big enough to get through.

They didn't appear to have any weapons, or fighting spirit, so I doubted they were anything to worry about. Still, I needed answers and they were the only ones that could give them to me.

I knocked on the glass. They looked at each other, exchanging words before one of the women came over to the glass.

"What's your name?"

"Suzette," the woman answered.

"Well, Suzette, if you open the door, I can get you outta here alive," I said.

She looked skeptical. "You can't expect me to believe that."

"If you aren't the one that's been cutting up folks then I can," I said. "You help me and I'll help you."

She motioned toward the other two with her head. "What about them?"

I looked past her at the two standing in the back of the room. "The real question is how bad do you want to live?"

"Nice try," she said.

There was a loud click and the doors shuddered in their tracks. They opened, leaving me standing face to face with Suzette. She jumped back so fast she tripped, falling in the middle of the room, but scrambling to her feet in a fraction of a second.

"I want to live," the other woman said, her hand on the door release.

"You fucking idiot," Suzette sneered. "He's going to kill us all."

<h1 style="text-align:center">CHAPTER · 28</h1>

"Cool your tits, Suzette," I said, stepping into the room.

She stood with the man against the wall.

I asked the woman who'd opened the door, "What's your name?"

"Jill." Her eyes went wide moving to something behind me. "Don't!"

Stabbing pain shot through my shoulder. The man who'd been standing behind the surgical table had buried a scalpel into my left shoulder. I spun in time to take another scalpel to the gut. I grabbed his wrist and twisted until his fingers were pointing toward the ceiling. The scalpel clattered to the floor. I jerked his hand down, sending him toppling to the floor with a pop from his wrist and a scream from his lips. He held his wrist to his chest. He looked up in time to catch my fist colliding with his face. He collapsed unconscious.

Suzette bolted out the open door, barreling down the hallway. Jill watched Suzette go, looked at me, and then back to Suzette. I could see her calculating her chances.

"Are you going to make a run for it, cause I could use some help with this," I said, holding a hand out to the scalpel buried in my shoulder.

I didn't really need help, but I needed Jill alive. If she followed Suzette she would be killed by the first member of the T.O. that found her.

"Did you mean what you said? You'll make sure we make it out alive?"

"No," I said. "I'll get *you* out alive. Suzette and Mr. Stabby are on their own."

Jill looked back down the corridor. Suzette made it to the end of the corridor just as Skinny Pete came around the corner. Jill turned away, putting a hand to her stomach, as Skinny Pete pounced.

She didn't look sure about hitching her horse to my wagon but must have decided I was her best chance.

"Sit on the table. I'll need sutures, antiseptic—"

"Just pull it," I said, turning to give her access.

She was hesitant but gave the scalpel a quick tug. "Did I hurt you?"

I rolled my shoulder a few times. "I'm fine. Stay close to me. If they catch you alone, I won't be able to protect you." I got a little of the blood from my shoulder and wiped it on her forehead. "It'll smell like me, might help."

She didn't look particularly happy, but didn't argue either. Skinny Pete came down the hallway dripping Suzette's blood from his mouth. He had a bit of flesh stuck in the hair on his chin. He looked at Jill the way a wolf looks at a sheep.

"She's with me," I said. I put a finger to my chin. "You've got a little something right there."

He swiped a couple fingers over his fur knocking the bit of Suzette free. "Did I get it?"

"Yep."

"I'm going to be sick." Jill moved her hand from her stomach to her mouth.

Skinny Pete looked down at the man just starting to stir on the ground. "And this one?"

I shrugged.

"Excellent," he grinned. "We've got company. Hank needs you

upstairs. I'll be right behind you." Skinny Pete stood over the man on the ground.

I took Jill by the arm and directed her out of the room. "Come on, we gotta move."

We barely made it out of the room before Skinny Pete tore into the man on the floor. Jill went from a brisk walk to a jog and then slowed down at the other side of the hallway when we came to Suzette's body. She tiptoed around the bloody body before we moved around the corner and up the stairs.

She stopped again at the bodies of the guards, staying out of the carnage lining the hallway. I could hear gunfire that sounded like it was coming from somewhere in the house above us. I almost passed the guards by, but with the sounds of gunfire I thought it might be good to have a little more range. I took two pistols and handed them to Jill. I scrounged a fresh magazine from the belt of one of the guards.

"You aren't afraid I'll shoot you?" Jill asked from behind me.

I moved to the other guard to see what he had on him. "I've found people act in their own interests. If you shoot me you'll be stuck with a bunch of pissed off shifters to deal with by yourself." I found a second magazine on the man's belt. I took it and turned around to face her. "Not to mention that you can't kill me with those. No matter how many times you shoot me I'll wake up. Needless to say, our deal will be off."

I reloaded the pistols before continuing down the hallway. I stopped when I realized Jill wasn't behind me anymore. When I looked I'd found she hadn't followed me past the guards bodies. She moved from one side of the hallway to the other looking for a way to get through without stepping in the gore. A futile exercise to say the least. I walked back through the mess, handed her the pistols, and crouched in front of her.

"Hop on," I said. "I'll carry you."

She climbed on my back and I stepped through the blood. When

I cleared, it rather than putting her down, I took off at a run down the hallway. I needed her but she was slowing me down and the T.O. needed my help.

I followed the sounds of fighting. I went up the flight of stairs into the house proper, stopping short of opening the door. I put Jill down and took the pistols.

"Stay safe but close," I said.

I cracked the door open and peered out. Through the kitchen, I saw the front door being covered by five people with guns and two standing on either side of the door. One was Torch, or another copy of him. I'd already taken one with his right arm and left leg. From what I saw in the cell this one had to be from a right leg. I didn't recognize the other man, but from his blank stare and lack of concern about the bullets flying back and forth, I had to assume he was a golem too. The T.O. couldn't get in without getting shot up. I could hear the Tortured Occult on the porch. I didn't think the guards had silver bullets, the guards I took the guns from didn't. Either way I was in a better position to even the playing field and get the T.O. in the house. I raised a pistol in each hand, holding them by my head and took a deep breath. This was gonna hurt.

I jumped into the kitchen, leveling the pistols at the guards. I charged, firing off as many rounds as I could. I wasn't aiming so much as just point-ing and shooting. Spray and pray, that was the name of the game. I hit a few of them before they realized what was happening. The golems moved to intercept me. My bullets slammed into them, tearing gashes into their bodies, exposing the earth they were made of. Dirt sprayed back on me as I closed in on them. The guards that hadn't been hit opened fire. It was lucky for me the golems had moved between us. They stopped most of the bullets intended for me. The ones they didn't stop went wide and missed me entirely.

The slides on the pistols locked open as I reached the kitchen counter.

I ducked below the counter for cover, dropped the pistols, and drew my blade. The Torch-golem came around the corner first. That was lucky for me because I knew what to target. I swung at its right leg as soon as it came around the corner. The blade cut through cleanly. The golem's leg was severed and it dissolved into a pile of dirt. I expected the other golem to come around the corner behind the first. I could easily get at least two swings and maybe kill it before it became a problem.

I held the blade at the ready, waiting for it to come around the corner, when hard cold hands grabbed me from above. The golem had reached over the counter. I didn't expect it to have that kind of foresight and I was about to pay for it. It grabbed my arm holding the blade with one hand. Its other hand held firmly against the back of my neck. I tried to kick free as it dragged me over the counter into the living room. The T.O. poured through the door. If they had taken a few seconds longer I'd be getting shot up about then. They made quick work of the remaining guards before turning their attention to the golem. Unfortunately, it wasn't going to stand still waiting to be destroyed. It slammed me down into the counter, my head contacting hard and the room went dark, sounds muffled. I could tell I was lying flat and something was off with my body but I couldn't tell what. Everything was numb.

I started to come out of the haze only to realize I was being stepped on and kicked. The T.O. were wrestling with the golem on top of me. I needed to crawl away, I didn't know what direction to go but anywhere had to be better than being trampled. I became aware my left arm wasn't working when I tried to move. I rolled.

The tunnel vision receded. The T.O. piled on the golem, pinning it against the counter. With two members on each arm and leg it looked like they were still having trouble keeping it under control. I could hear muffled shouting but couldn't make out what they were saying. It looked like they were having trouble finding the piece the golem was made from.

Ginsu jumped up on the counter behind the golem and sunk his claws into its head under the jaw. He pulled as if he were doing a deadlift. The head ripped free. The body disintegrated into dust, leaving Ginsu holding a head. He tossed it into the living room. It rolled to a stop a few feet from me.

Mila knelt in front of me. "You alright? You gotta nose bleed."

"Yeah," I said, running an arm across my nose to wipe the blood away. "I got my bell rung. I'll be fine."

Big Ticket dragged Jill by the arm and threw her to the floor. She rolled to a stop, realized she was lying on a dismembered head, and scooted away like a crab only to discover she was surrounded by bikers with nowhere to go.

CHAPTER • 29

"She's with me," I said, getting to my feet.

My head hadn't quite cleared and I stumbled a little from the dizziness.

"You can't save everybody," Hank said.

I helped Jill up by the arm and pulled her behind me. "I'm not trying to save everybody. Just this one."

"You better have a good reason after what they did to Torch," Hank sneered.

"Because we haven't found Holt. I need to figure out what happened to him and she's going to tell me."

Hank's expression softened a bit. "Alright, but she comes back to the clubhouse and if she doesn't come through, she's ours."

"Agreed."

Hank turned to the club. "Secure this fucking place and find out what happened to the group that should have cleared the house."

"Up here," Cotton shouted from the top of the stairs. "They're shot up."

Mila headed for the stairs. "I got it."

"Obie, take her to the cells and get Torch out," Hank said. "Get 'em both to the clubhouse."

I took Jill by the arm and headed for the stairs.

"What the hell was that?" She said when we'd made it into the hall-way. "We had a deal now you're going to hand me over to them?"

We reached the massacre in the hallway. I bent down so Jill could get on my back. "We still have a deal. If you come through you'll be fine."

She climbed on to avoid the gore. "There's a lot of them and one of you. If they decide they want to hurt me you can't stop them. You're just handing me over to them."

I put her down when we passed the blood. "Hank gave us his word. That may not mean much for most folks but his word is good."

"You'll have to forgive me if I'm skeptical," Jill said.

We made it to the cells.

I looked at the prisoners through the glass. "We aren't going to be able to fit everyone in the truck. Do they have a van or something we can move everyone in?"

Jill pointed down the hallway. "There's an elevator that goes up to a separate garage. They have an ambulance parked there. We'll need a gurney to move thirty-sev— uh, Torch . . . We have one in storage."

"Alright, show me how to open these doors."

Jill pressed a button on the bottom of the panel. "The release is here then pull this," she said, pulling a large lever down.

I could hear the discharge of air of the room's pressure being equalized followed by a heavy locking mechanism being disengaged. She pulled the handle and the door swung open freely.

"Listen . . . Taking Torch is fine but you should probably leave every-one else where they are. They're dangerous."

"We can't just leave them," Mila said.

She had followed us down the stairs.

"Everyone okay up there?" I asked.

"Just some cuts and bullet wounds," Mila said. "They'll be fine."

"If no one is going to be here to take care of them then we should kill them," Jill said. "A number of the experiments escaped with Torch when he broke out. It's not good for them, or anyone else, to have them running around."

Mila crossed her arms. "We're taking everyone with us."

"Hold on . . ." I said holding up a hand. "Atticus wants to come back, under different management of course. She's right, we can't take 'em all with us. Let's get Torch now. We'll have to figure out what to do with the rest later."

Mila crossed her arms. "Fine, but I don't like it."

"Noted," I said. "Let's get that gurney."

Jill led me to a storage room. It contained metal shelves stacked with neatly labeled medical supplies. A clipboard with an inventory sheet was hanging off the closest shelf. Say what you will, they were organized.

Jill fetched a gurney. "Who is that?"

"A friend of mine. She's cool."

"Is she like . . . them?" Jill asked.

"She's like me."

I was sure she didn't know what that meant but she didn't ask any more questions. We rolled the gurney back to Torch's cell. Mila was standing by the open door.

"He told me to leave him alone."

"Alright, hang on." I stepped past her into the cell. "Hey, buddy, We're here to take you home."

He looked up at me for the first time. It was as if someone had taken all the fight out of him. His eyelids and mouth drooped, making him look sickly, which he probably was.

"Obie, we've been friends my whole life. I'd like to think we're close."

"Yeah, of course we are," I said. "Where are you going with this?"

"I need you to do something for me, no questions asked."

I walked over and knelt in front of him. "What?"

"Kill me."

I was afraid he was going to ask something like that. I'm a firm believer in a person's right to choose how they live, or not live as they case may be, but this wasn't the time for him to make that decision.

"I'll make you a deal. Come to the clubhouse and learn what life will be like for you. In six months if you still don't believe you have a future then I'll help you."

"What kind of future could I have? They didn't just take my limbs, they took my life. I can't ride anymore."

"You're still part of the club," I said. "I know the T.O. isn't going to turn its back on you."

"I'm not going to be a charity-case hang-around that everyone feels sorry for. I'd rather die."

"And if you still feel that way in six months then we'll talk," I said. "It's the best offer you're going to get."

"Fine." He looked at the floor. "It's not like I have a choice."

I brought in the gurney and placed him on it. We wheeled him into the hallway.

I walked over to Jessie's cell. Oreo started yapping.

"Did they do anything to your newest addition here?" I asked.

Jull shook her head. "She just got here."

I opened the door to her cell. The sprinklers were still on. She and Oreo came out of the cell dripping wet. While the water hadn't improved her spirits it had whittled away at some of the tar.

"Let's get you outta here," I said.

She sneered at me as she walked past. We wheeled Torch down the hall to the elevator. We took it up to the garage. Mila found the keys to the ambulance while we loaded Torch in the back. Jill, Jessie, and Oreo climbed in with Torch.

I got in the passenger seat. "Alright, let's roll. Drop me at my truck. Hopefully its still in one piece."

When we got to the gas station we found everything was quiet. The prospects were lounging lazily around the bikes. My truck wasn't burned to a crisp. That was a good sign. Mila pulled the ambulance in beside my truck. The back of the ambulance opened. I thought it was Jill making a run for it. I jumped out and went around to find Jessie standing by the back door.

"What're you doing?" I asked.

"Take me home."

"It may not be safe for you there. They know where your house is."

She jabbed a finger into my chest. "And who's fault is that?"

"I'm not gonna be able to protect you if something happens."

"'Cause you're doing a bang up job of that already?" she asked.

I held a hand out directing her to my truck. "We'll meet you at the clubhouse," I said to Mila before closing the ambulance door.

The truck looked to be in good shape. The windows were down but Atticus wasn't in it.

He walked out of the shadows beside the gas station. "How'd it go?"

"Pretty good," I said. "Get in, we need to get back."

He got in the back. "Who's this?"

I started the truck. "A friend, we're taking her home."

"We're not friends," Jessie said.

"Where's my car?" she said when we pulled up to her house.

It was the first thing she noticed.

"Last time I saw it, it was on fire on the side of seventy five," I said.

She got out of the truck, sat Oreo down, and turned to me. "Obie, in the future, should you find yourself in trouble, don't come to me."

I nodded. "That's fair."

CHAPTER 30

"We're headed south," Atticus said.

"We are."

"The facility's north."

"It is," I agreed.

"So where are we going?"

I could feel the temperature in the truck start to rise with his anxiety. "You promised me you would take me back and put me in a cell."

"And I will," I said. "I'm trying to look out for you. The Tortured Occult is watching the facility but we don't know if they are going to try to take it back and we need to get some more people over there to help out. On top of that I saw one of the staff making a phone call. There could be a team coming to retake the facility right now. If you want to go back before we feel we can protect you, then I'll take you. You could end up right back where you started."

"How long will I have to wait?" he asked.

"A day, two tops."

He took a deep breath. "Let's hope for a day."

I caught up to the ambulance twenty minutes before we got to Morrison Salvage. Doc Lin was waiting for us at the clubhouse. Looking sour, she leaned against her Mercedes. Mila backed the ambulance up to the back door. I parked the truck and went to talk to Doc Lin.

"Thanks for coming," I said.

She crossed her arms. "Did I have a choice?"

"If you'll accept the consequences you can make any choice you want." I said, opening the ambulance doors.

Her attitude changed when she saw the condition Torch was in. We pulled him out of the ambulance and took him to one of the bedrooms. We put him on the bed and I left Doc Lin and Jill alone with him as I took the gurney back to the ambulance. Hank, Big Ticket, and Cotton rolled up as I was loading it.

Hank pulled up beside me. "Where is he?"

"In the back. Doc Lin and Jill are checking him out."

I followed him to Torch's room.

"Well?" Hank asked. "What d'ya think?"

Doc Lin finished inspecting Torch. "He's got a fever. From what I know of ultranatural physiology he should have healed by now. He's really not doing well. He should be in a hospital."

"Unfortunately, that's not an option," I said. "Just do your best."

She snapped the latex gloves off her hands and tossed them into the trash. "I don't need you to tell me how to do my job."

It's the first time she'd snapped at me. I wasn't going to make a big deal about it. She was probably upset about everything that happened with her husband. I wasn't sure she made up her mind if she was still going to pursue working with the ultranatural community. We needed her and she came, that was enough for now.

"Fair enough," I said. "Do you need Jill for anything?"

"I'm fine."

I opened the door and held it. "Jill," I said. "It's time we had a chat."

I led her into another room and closed the door. She stood on the far side of the room while I stood in front of the door.

"Listen, I'm not gonna lie to you, you're in a bad spot. I'm sure you don't know anything about number thirty-seven but he's a member of the Tortured Occult Motorcycle Club. The leader's son. I go back with Hank and the club a long time, since its inception. All this is to say, I have some pull. I'm sure Hank will want to talk to you and if you get out of here in one piece or not depends on how you speak to him so keep that in mind. I'll do what I can for you and in return, I need to know only one thing. Where is Holt?"

Jill shrugged. "I don't know who Holt is. They have numbers, not names. What did he look like?"

I hadn't taken any pictures of Holt. We weren't the kind of guys that stood around taking selfies. Hell, I just learned what a selfie was.

"He's a Doberman. Seven feet tall with black fur."

"Ah," Jill said. "I saw him. He wasn't like the others. I don't know what but there was something special about him. He was only at the facility for about a day. Dr. Tsukimora took him from the facility about an hour before you showed up."

"Took him where?"

"I heard him mention the Nacoochee Mound to his guards. I don't know what it is though."

I headed for the door. "I do."

A crash and yelling erupted from the bar.

"Come on, something's up," I said.

Jill followed me into the hallway. We ran into Mila and Atticus.

"What's she doing here?" Atticus asked.

I could feel the temperature start to rise.

Jill backed down the hallway away from him.

"What was the noise?" I asked, moving to the bar.

Just as I put my hand on the door it crashed in on me, throwing me against the wall and knocking me to the ground. A tar cat stood in the hallway. It was the size of a Saint Bernard. Its body glistened and churned. Jill ran out the back when she saw it.

If it had jumped on me there would have been nothing I could've done to defend myself. It was looking at Mila and Atticus. It charged them before I could get to my feet. Mila pushed Atticus down the hall. There was no chance they could outrun it and, in the confines of the hallway, Mila couldn't outmaneuver it either. The tar cat charged. It leapt for Mila. She dropped to the floor avoiding it. It collided with Atticus instead.

Flames erupted, engulfing the end of the hallway. I raised a hand to shield my eyes from the heat. I couldn't see any trace of Atticus or Mila. I got to my feet.

I burst through the first door on my right and almost ran into Doc Lin.

"What's happening?" she asked.

"The clubhouse is on fire, I'll get Torch, you get out now."

She disappeared into the hallway.

Torch tried to push me away as I bent down to pick him up. "Just leave me here," he said. "Save yourself."

"We're not going over this again," I said, pushing his hand out of the way and hoisting him up.

The flames had already made it halfway down the hall by the time I got Torch out of the room. In the bar one of the Tortured Occult, I couldn't tell who, writhed on the floor, covered in tar. Most of the patrons had already made a beeline for the exit. Hank and Big Ticket were standing by helplessly watching the tar suffocate their brother.

Hank yelled, "What the fuck's going on?"

"Fire," I said. "Get Torch out."

Hank took him from me and headed for the exit. No sooner had I spoken than the tar assumed the shape of a cat, revealing Cotton gasping for breath on the floor. The cat prowled toward me. Big Ticket scooped Cotton off the floor.

"Fire extinguishers?" I shouted.

Big Ticket pulled Cotton's arm over his shoulder. "Behind the bar."

"Get out," I shouted. "I'm right behind you."

I backed away from the tar cat. I didn't know if a fire extinguisher would do any good against it, I doubted it. I didn't bother to draw my blade. It wasn't going to do any good. I was back to the problem I had at Eddy's trailer; How do you fight a liquid?

I was surprised the tar cat hadn't attacked. It prowled towards me as if it was trying to back me into a corner. I'd decided to make a run for it when the door to the back burst open, dumping flames into the bar. The tar cat was immediately engulfed. It writhed in on itself as it caught fire. The new fuel source made the bar catch that much faster. I could feel my whiskers singeing from the heat. I jumped over the bar, landing hard on the floor.

While it only took a few seconds to find the fire extinguishers, I realized that there was an exorbitant amount of high proof alcohol lining the wall behind me. With the amount of heat coming over the top of the bar, it wouldn't be long before the booze went up as well. I'd jumped out of the frying pan and into the fire.

"Obie," a voice said from the flames.

I didn't recognize it. I peeked over the bar. I had to squint to see Atticus standing in the middle of the room. It wasn't that he was on fire, it's as if he was fire itself.

He took a step toward me. "You should've taken me back."

I pulled the pin on a fire extinguisher. I gave him a blast. He roared like an inferno and fell back, disappearing into a white cloud. I emptied the entire can into the room. It didn't put out the flames, but did push them back. I coughed from the smoke. I put my head to the floor and took a deep breath. I could hold my breath for about ten minutes. It should be more than enough to get out, if the fire didn't get me first.

Big Ticket came through the door to the changing room. "Come on, Obie, this place is coming down."

He didn't realize there was a werewolf made of fire standing in the room until Atticus turned toward him. He strode forward leaving flaming footprints on the wood floor. The fire department would be here soon. If they found Atticus, a lot of fire fighters would die. Then again they were probably better equipped to fight him than I was. Either way, the survivors would become aware that the world is a little more diverse than they thought. I had to take care of him quick.

I pulled my blade and jumped over the bar. Atticus's flaming figure was standing in the doorway to the changing room which was now engulfed. It was my only way out. I charged into the heat, slashing into his back. My blade passed through the center of his body with little resistance. It didn't seem to slow him down one bit. He spun around swinging a flaming arm at me. I ducked under it, barely avoiding the strike. The smell of singed fur filled my nose. I dove away and rolled to a table. There were some unfinished drinks on top. I picked them up one by one and hurled them at Atticus. I didn't hit with all of them but the ones that did just evaporated like a drop of water on a hot skillet. I threw a chair at him and it went through his body, crashing to the floor, engulfed in flames.

Atticus raised his arms over his head and brought them crashing down on me. I dove under the table. As he hit the table flames poured over the sides. I closed my eyes tight to protect them from the heat. It seemed like the whole world was on fire. I dove out from under the table and got to my feet in time to see Atticus spinning with an arm extended. The result was a wave of flame sweeping in my direction. I rolled over the bar, falling onto the floor as the wave crashed into it sending flames and broken glasses raining down on me.

I pulled a zip tie from my pocket. Grabbing the other extinguisher, I pulled the pin and zip tied the handle. I was granted an immediate reprieve from the heat and I was grateful to have it. I didn't have long before it would run out but it gave me a few seconds to come up with another plan. I tossed the extinguisher over the bar like an anti-fire grenade, knocking the soda gun off its hook.

The nozzle of the soda gun fell from the bar into my lap. Atticus said that water had put the flame out the first time he ignited. If I could get him back into his normal physical form, he would be easy to deal with.

I jumped up, pointed the soda gun at Atticus, and pushed a button. I expected the kind of powered stream from a carbonated water dispenser you see on The Three Stooges. What I got was a flaccid stream that went about a foot forward on the bar.

Atticus sent a wave of flame, engulfing the arm holding the soda gun. I dropped it and fell back behind the bar clutching my charred appendage to my chest. It hurt too much to scream and if I had I would have lost all my air. I figured that was it for me. If it was just me in a burning building, I could make it out. With Atticus between me and the door there was nothing I could do.

If I'd had my druthers, I would have died of smoke inhalation. Burning alive was gonna be a bitch, and considering how fast I healed, it would take much longer than a human. That was a bad way to go, but that's the life of a Keeper. We don't get happy endings.

Bottles of liquor exploded, raining down glass and fire. I couldn't avoid it, I had nowhere to go. I thought about exhaling and getting a big breath of smoke. I could put my blade through my chest and at least be unconscious for the inevitable. I pulled my blade and lined it up with the tip over my heart. Just one strong pull, and it would all be over.

A new commotion in the room. The roar of the fire transitioned into a scream of agony. Water splashed over the bar, accompanied by the sound of a fire being quenched. Steam clouds rolled. I peeked out. Fire fighters stood in the doorway to the changing room. They held a large hose that sprayed a steady stream of water into Atticus. I couldn't let them see me in krasis so I changed back to my human form, but kept my blade handy.

It wasn't enough to put him out, but where the water hit he phased back into physical form. He reignited when the stream moved away. I waited until the water hit him again and swung for the fences. I couldn't tell where I hit him but the blade bit into something solid. By the third hit there was no trace of him. I ran through the steam and smoke to make my escape.

CHAPTER • 31

Outside the clubhouse, I exhaled the breath I had been holding and took in fresh air through clenched teeth. My left arm was missing skin in some places, was black in others. It was a mess and hurt like hell to boot.

A fireman carrying an oxygen tank ran up to me. He stopped in his tracks when he saw my arm. Then he looked at my blade and up to my grimacing face.

"Thanks," I said. "I'm alright."

The fireman held his hands up, making it clear he wasn't going to argue. The fire chief was talking to Hank by one of the fire trucks on the scene.

The chief cut the conversation short. "Get everybody out," he yelled. "We've got ammunition inside. Get everybody down to the road."

I slid into the ambulance's driver seat. I tossed my blade on the passenger seat, rested my charred left arm in my lap, and cranked the engine. I moved the ambulance to a safe distance, put it in park, and closed my eyes. I sat and breathed, needing a few minutes for the pain to subside. A tap on my window. I opened my eyes to see Hank. I reached over with my right hand to lower the window.

"Jill ran off."

I sighed. "Just let her go. It's not like she can expose the clubhouse now."

"You alright?" Hank asked.

I nodded. "I will be. Just need to sit for a few minutes and then I'm going after Holt. Jill gave me a lead before everything went to shit."

"Where's Mila?" He asked.

I shook my head. "She was in the hallway where the fire started. I don't think she made it out."

"You need help with Holt?"

I shifted to try and find a position that didn't hurt. "You should stay here and deal with the clubhouse. I'll handle it."

"Alright," he said patting a hand on the door. "Go get him."

It still hurt like hell, but I needed to get on the road. I threw the ambulance in drive and headed north to the Nacoochee Indian Mound.

I arrived just after sundown. The mound was in the middle of a field flanked on two sides by roads with forest in the back. A wire fence around the field and another at the base of the mound kept out the public. It was little more than a large earthen mound constructed by indigenous people long before my time. A gazebo had been built on the top. I couldn't make out anyone on top of the mound or in the gazebo, it was too dark, but that didn't mean they weren't there. I needed a stealthy approach and an ambulance wasn't the most discreet vehicle.

I drove past the mound and pulled off on the side of the road where the ambulance would be obscured by the forest. I checked out my arm. It still looked like hell but I could move it again. I grabbed my blade from the passenger seat and walked into the woods to make the change to krasis. Securing the blade in its sheath, I crept up close enough to the tree line to get a look at the mound. I sat for a few minutes and watched. I didn't see any movement or hear any noise coming from the mound. I took off my clothes, took the form of an otter, and headed for the mound.

I had to maneuver a field of cows and cowpies. Halfway through the field the wind shifted and I got a whiff of humans. There were a few dark figures on the top of the mound silhouetted against the night sky. Getting under the fence was easy. Getting to the top would prove more difficult.

"There's something down there," a woman said.

I crouched low and still.

It was quiet for a few seconds before a man answered. "I don't see anything."

"Something small, it ducked into the grass at the bottom of the hill."

"We're almost done," the man said. "Shoot anything that moves."

I poked my head up until I could see through the grass. Two figures were looking down in my direction. Rifle barrels stuck out from their sides. The little bit of light from passing cars reflected off something on their faces—night vision goggles. This was going to get hairy. I heard a *pfft pfft*. Something whizzed past me. It took me a second to realize what was happening. They were using silencers. I ducked back into the grass. Cows behind me trotted farther away.

There was no way up without taking fire, not after I was spotted. Maybe I should have taken Hank up on his offer for help. I would just have to make a run for it.

Someone started reciting an incantation in the gazebo. I didn't know the spell but I recognized the voice, I just couldn't place it.

"Obie." Thera was suddenly standing beside me. "Stop this now. I won't be contained again."

"What do you mean again?" I said in otter squeaks.

"What the fuck is that?" the man on top of the mound asked.

"It's like before, when I was trapped in Holt," she said. "Stop it now."

"I have to find a way to get up there safely," I said. "If you could give me a lightning strike just over there it would blind them and I—"

"You're out of favors and time. Take your real form and go now," Thera commanded.

"Look, if I go now I'll—"

Thera put a finger to my forehead and forced my body into krasis. The shooting started almost immediately. I took a bullet in the leg and one in the shoulder before I could get moving. I did my best to be hard to hit but there was no cover available and moving uphill slowed me down. Not as much as the bullets, mind you, but it was all working against me. I made it halfway up the hill before I took a shot to the gut then another to the chest before everything went black.

I woke with a face full of grass. My body ached in the many places I'd been shot. I picked my head up and looked around. I had been carried up to the top of the mound, just outside the gazebo.

"He's waking up," the man said.

"If he makes any sudden moves, shoot him again," the familiar voice said. "Obie, please just stay still. This is only going to take a few minutes more."

Inside the gazebo Holt was laid out on the floor in a circle, just like the time when Petra had captured him in the apartment building. A man knelt over him, a man I knew. I couldn't believe what I was seeing.

"Travis? Is that you?"

He smiled at me. "You don't recognize me? I can't say I blame you. I'm not wearing rags and speaking like some backwoods hick. Let me introduce myself again, Travis Tsukimora. Nice to meet you for real."

"You're a real son of a bitch."

"Don't be like that," Travis said. "You're not really mad at me, you're mad at yourself for not figuring it out."

"No, I'm mad at you."

"I have to admit, I like you, Obie. I thought I was going to have to use you for this, but you got a new apprentice. I have to say I'm glad."

I got slowly on my knees. "Use me anyway. Let Holt go."

"I'm not going to do that."

"Why the hell not? Why do you care?"

Travis put a small box on the ground beside Holt and opened it. "You pretended to drink the water."

"What the hell are you talking about?"

Travis laughed and ran a hand over his head. "When you came to see me a couple days ago. I thought you figured it out! You actually caught me alone. I thought I was in real trouble but I threw on the overalls and donned the hick talk and you were clueless. You even said something about how the shirt didn't match." Travis shook his head and walked around to the other side of the circle. "I brought you water in the first glass I could find. I don't even use that one, I have clean ones downstairs. That came with the house."

"Is there a point to all this?"

"I have cameras all over the property. I saw you pour out some of the water and press it to your lip. You did that to protect my feelings, Obie. My fucking feelings! Jesus! Who acts like that?"

"So, you didn't use me because I was nice to you?"

Travis shrugged. "Long and short of it, yes. The world's in short supply of good people and you're good people. I'd feel bad doing this to you. Don't get me wrong, I'd still do it if I didn't have another option, but I do, so no problem."

I looked over my shoulder. The two guards pointed rifles at me. "Yes, problem. What's the point of all this anyway, to kill Thera?"

"I don't think it's possible to kill Thera." Travis chuckled. "It's nothing so devious. I'm part of an organization whose purpose is to find a way to practice magic without dust."

I sighed. "You can't practice magic without dust. It's impossible. People have tried."

"Harlan found a way to do it, although it didn't end well for him."

"How do you even know about that?" I asked.

"I know a lot of things," he said. "He made a deal with the devil, so to speak, not what I had in mind. Have you heard of ley lines?" He didn't wait for me to answer. "They're veins of magical energy running through the earth. The problem is, they are inaccessible. If we can tap into those lines, we can practice magic without dust. Do you realize what that means? No more hunting. Your friends won't have to look over their shoulders anymore."

"Don't pretend you're doing this as a kindness," I spat. "How many of my friends have you killed trying to make this happen?"

"Many I'm afraid and I'm sorry about that. Let's cut the bullshit, Obie. People like to pretend that the ends don't justify the means, but they do. The winners write history and when it's all said and done, no one cares how progress is made. Sure, people will piss and moan for a bit and then they forget."

"I won't forget," I said.

Travis pulled a knife in the shape of a talon out of the box. "I know you won't, Obie. When this is all over, if you want to come after me . . . Well, let's just say I expect it. You'll have a hard time finding me though. I don't plan to stick around when this is done."

"Time's on my side," I said. "I can invest as many years as it takes to find you."

"That's true, you can. But I think you won't. I'm putting money down that when this is all over you won't come after me at all."

"I'll take that bet," I said.

Travis held up the knife and knelt beside Holt. "I suspect when this is all said and done you won't be a Keeper anymore, just a normal shifter. If I'm right, that means you won't be silver immune. I told you I like you and I meant it. I don't expect you to sit there and watch but if they shoot you with those silver bullets it will probably kill you in a few minutes." He reached inside his jacket and pulled out a revolver. "These are just lead." He pointed the gun at me and pulled the trigger.

When I woke, it was still dark. The ground was soft from blood. Head-shots were the worst. My head felt like a smashed watermelon. I put a hand to my temple. It was just Holt and I alone on the mount. Travis and his lackies had split while I was unconscious.

I rubbed my eyes and got to my feet. "Holt, you awake yet?"

He was lying on his back in the middle of a circle drawn on the ground. Half empty crates of dust had been left around him. His fore-arms had long cuts running from his wrists to the crook of his elbow. I didn't know how long I had been out, but Holt should have healed by now. I held my hand over his arm and channeled energy into him—at least I tried to. The energy flowed over him instead of healing his cuts. I touched his arm. He was cold. I watched the cuts on his arm for any sign they were healing.

After a couple minutes I fell back into a seated position. "I'm sorry, Holt."

CHAPTER · 32

I loaded Holt's body in the ambulance and took him home. I made some calls and got to work building a funeral pyre. I dug a pit and collected all the firewood I had on hand. I'd never built a funeral pyre before and I wasn't sure exactly how large it should be. I figured too large was better than too small and piled the wood wide and high. It took me all morning. I kept checking periodically throughout the day to see if he had miraculously started healing. He hadn't. I put his body on the pyre, placing his arms by his sides to hide the cuts.

When I was done I sat in front of the pyre, staring at my failure. Mila had lived through the fire but wasn't in good shape. When Atticus ignited, it killed the tar cat almost instantly. Unfortunately, Mila had been covered in burning tar. She made it out the back and collapsed between some cars in the junkyard. The T.O. had found her in the morning.

I'd arranged for her to stay with my friend Livy while she healed. I'd known Livy most of my life. It was a different kind of magic that had kept her alive. Her home was secluded in the woods. A perfect spot for a recovering Keeper to stay out of sight.

I heard a car pull up to the house. A few minutes later someone walked up behind me. I didn't want to talk to anyone. I knew I was about to be on the receiving end of a steady stream of pity.

"You're gonna have to help me sit," Livy said. "I don't get up and down as easy as I used to."

I held out a hand. She eased down beside me. She was my oldest friend and the only person that I could tolerate right now.

We sat quietly for a few minutes before she spoke. "What's the matter, hun?"

"Maybe it's my dead friend up there," I said, holding a hand out to the pyre. "That's a stupid question."

Livy shifted her weight from side to side. "I swannie," she mumbled to herself.

That may not seem like a lot but for Livy that was as close to cursing as she got. I'd hurt her feelings and now I felt like a dick.

I sighed. "Look, I'm sorry. This has been rough on me."

"I've buried all my family and most of my friends," she said, putting a hand on my knee. "It will be my turn soon and if I'm being honest, I'm ready. It's hard being old. You hurt all the time. I know that you've lost a lot of people, too, and I know that you're taking this one hard but you still have people that care about you. You don't have to do this alone."

"For the last time, we're the same age," I said.

Livy patted my knee with her wrinkled hand. "We're the same age, but you aren't old."

She was right of course. I hadn't experienced the past two hundred years the same way she had. I'd never know what it was to grow old, at least I thought. Travis's words stuck in my mind: *just a normal shifter.* If he was right, the clock could have just started for me. I'd watched Livy grow old and feeble. Gray hair, wrinkled face, arthritic hands . . . could that be me? I found the idea strangely comforting.

"What I was saying was that you've got a lot of people here for you," she continued. "I expect you to be upset, I just don't want you to think you have to go through this alone."

I sighed. "I hear you and I appreciate it. This really got to me because it didn't have to happen. I could have saved him but I was prevented from doing it . . . twice."

"I'm not one to tell someone how to feel. Go ahead and be angry if you need to," she said. "Just keep lookin' forward."

Our friends began showing up in the evening. Mila decided to wait in the house until everyone had left, I didn't blame her. The T.O. was first to arrive. They rolled in on their motorcycles followed by the van. I went up to greet them as they were taking a wheelchair out of the back of the van. They took it to the passenger side and helped Torch into it. He looked like hell.

Hank was the first to greet me. "Can we do anything to help?"

"There's some chairs in the barn if you could set them out for folks," I said. "And . . . don't mind the bodies and junk. I haven't had a chance to pick up."

I hadn't had a chance to dispose of the bodies and equipment we'd brought back from Eirene.

He grinned. "Sure."

I tipped my head toward Torch. "How's he doing?"

"His body's healing fast, faster than I expected to be honest, but he's not doing well," Hank said. "We'll get those chairs for you."

Queen Isabelle came next with Yarwor, Hob, and a procession of elves. I thanked them one by one but noticed Hob had stayed back waiting to talk to me last. I shook hands and gave them all sad smiles. When the procession had finally passed, Hob came up to me.

"Something is different," he said.

"What are we talking about?"

He raised a hand and snapped his fingers leaving his thumb pointing up. On the tip of his thumb a flame the size of a candle burned. He didn't have any dust, at least none I could see. Travis had said his mission was to have magic without the restriction of dust . . . Could his plan have worked?

I cocked my head. "How'd you do that?"

"It is the same process but without dust. I can feel an energy move through *mine* body," he said.

I wondered if it was the same way I felt the energy move when I healed people. I had no way to know.

"I have a lot to tell you. I'll come up tomorrow and we'll see if we can't figure it out," I said.

Holt had only been in north Georgia for about six months but he had a good turnout; the Tortured Occult, Hambone, and more ultras than I could shake a stick at. When everyone had paid their respects, I lit the pyre. We all stood around watching it burn and listening to stories about Holt. He'd made friends with more of these people than I'd realized. He was a goofball and kind of a screw up, but he was kind and loyal and brave. They all loved him for it, and so did I. He'd made a big impact in such a short time and found a home and a family here.

By the time the pyre had burned down to embers the only ones left were Keepers. Mila came out of the house and joined us. Even in the dim light of the fire I could see the damage that had been done to her body. It was gruesome.

Cearbhall had come up from Jekyll. They were the only two Keepers I knew well but all Keepers shared a bond of brotherhood that made them instant family. I'd filled them in on what happened earlier. We sat quietly for a while, no one wanting to break the silence. The orange glow of the embers lit our faces, accentuating our connectedness to Holt and each other.

Babatunde, a hyena from Africa who'd moved to Virginia a few years back, was the first to speak. "So, what are we going to do about Thera?"

"What's there to do?" Cearbhall asked. "We don't even know what happened to her."

Drool drizzled out of a hole in Mila's cheek and onto some exposed bone in her arm as she spoke. "Obie, what do you think happened."

I tapped my fingers on my leg. "Well, I'm no expert. Travis said he linked or connected Holt to Thera. I think that when he . . . cut Holt that it sort of cut Thera as well. He wanted to open the ley lines, flood the world with magic. He said the ley lines were like magical veins running through the earth. He opened Holt's veins and spilled his blood, by extension he cut Thera and spilled hers. I think it worked. Hob can do at least basic magic without dust now. He showed me earlier."

"So, Thera's injured then," Roscoe said. He was a werewolf from Louisiana.

"It stands to reason," Cearbhall said. "But again, what are we going to do about it? How do you heal the Earth Mother?"

"Travis said he was part of an organization that had been working on opening the ley lines," I said.

Roscoe sounded excited. "Then they would know best how to reverse what he did."

"Sure," I said. "If we can find them. I may not have his real name. It turns out I didn't know him at all."

"It might be worth looking into," Babatunde said.

"We need to talk about if we want to put things back the way they were," Mila said.

"Why the hell wouldn't we?" Roscoe said.

Mila eased back in the wheelchair she was using while her body recovered. "Thera doesn't care about us. I didn't realize the extent of it until I met Eirene. We're tools to Thera. Expendable. I used to think that's the way her kind was but it's not true. She's cold and self-absorbed."

Roscoe looked angry. "You shouldn't talk about her like that."

"No, I haven't been *able* to talk about her like that," Mila said. "It was a crime to even think things like that before now. I'm free for the first time and I'm not feeling motivated to go back. We should be asking ourselves if Thera deserves our loyalty."

"She has mine," Roscoe said. "And you might want to think about what she'll do when she comes back. What if we don't do anything and she wakes up in a month. Where will you be then?"

Babatunde nodded. "That's a good point. We don't even know how permanent this is."

Cearbhall sighed. "How long have you been doing this, Roscoe?"

"I became a Keeper in 1934."

Cearbhall nodded. "You're still a puppy. I've been doing this longer than anyone here. I remember the Roman invasion in Ireland. I've dedicated over two millennium to Thera's service. I've lost countless friends and an eye in the process. I'm tired."

"I can't believe what I'm hearing!" Roscoe shouted. "We owe our lives to her. I don't care what any of you say. I'm going to do everything in my power to restore Thera. I feel sorry for any of you that are on the wrong side of things when she's back. I guess it's just me and Obie. Right, Obie?"

Everyone looked at me. "Holt should still be alive. When I tried to save him the other night Thera intervened, sent me on another job. Then when I had found him she forced a change on me that got me shot and captured. I don't know if I would have been able to save him . . . I do know I would have at least had a chance. Cearbhall was a better father to me than I deserved. He taught me everything I know. I've seen the toll first hand being a Keeper's taken on him. I also think of Walasi buried in a hillside alone like trash thrown out on the side of the road. There's no future in service to Thera, only pain and misery." I took a deep breath. "I've been giving this a lot of thought. No one can tell another what to do. If you want to try and save Thera then good luck to you. I won't be helping."

Roscoe stood. "You're all a bunch of cowards. If you aren't going to do the right thing then there's nothing else to discuss."

He stormed away into the night. I didn't blame him for his reaction. I'd been gung-ho in my younger days too. It was easier back then, everything was black and white. Whatever Thera said was right. Do what you're told and don't ask questions. I hadn't felt that way in a long time.

"What about Travis?" Babatunde asked.

"We can do something about Travis, if we can find him," I said. "I'll put feelers out. He's out there somewhere, it's a matter of time before he turns up. When he does, I'll handle it."

CHAPTER · 33

Hank's house was a single-story brick ranch tucked away in the woods. I pulled up a little before noon. I got out to find Hank's cupita, Marge, working in her garden. She stood when she heard the truck coming. I gave her a wave as I got out of the truck and got one back. On the way to the front door I saw two young black bears peeking out at me from behind a pickup. They were Hank's two youngest, Joel and Adaline. I pretended not to notice them as I walked to the door.

When I had just gotten past them they charged. Joel, the younger of the two, went for my legs while Adaline jumped on my back. Joel wrapped around my right leg, which let me brace enough to not be knocked over.

I thrashed around in feigned panic and shouted, "Oh no! I'm being attacked by vicious bears!"

Hank came out of the house. "Get off him. You're supposed to be helping your mother in the garden."

Adaline jumped off my back and ran off in the opposite direction of the garden. I looked down at Joel who still had my leg in his mouth. He looked up at me.

Hank said, "Spit him out already. You've got to stop doing this to every person that comes over."

Joel ran off after his sister.

"Those kids'll be the death of me. Just about gave the mailman a heart attack last week. I told Marge to have her Amazon orders sent to the shop from now on," Hank said, shaking his head. "So, what can I do for ya?"

"I came for Torch. I thought of a way we might be able to get him some legs. I don't know if it will work, but I was on the phone with Hob this morning and he thinks it's worth a shot."

"You can talk to him . . . see if you can convince him," Hank said.

"You don't think he'd go for it?"

Hank put his hands on his hips. "If I'm being honest, I barely recognize him. Torch didn't come back. We got a shell of the person he was. But go try."

I walked past him into the house. I found Torch in the living room, staring at a blank television.

"Hey, Torch, I'm gonna cut to the chase here. I think I found a way to get you a new arm and legs. I came over to see if it's something you're interested in."

He was quiet for a few seconds. "Like prosthetics? Hunks of plastic that don't do anything but make me look more normal?"

I sat on a chair across from him. "Kinda, but fully functional limbs, and no plastic."

"How?"

"Magic," I said. "Hob thinks we can do it."

"There's no dust, or at least not enough."

"We don't need it anymore." I leaned forward to emphasize the point. "After everything that's happened I think we could both use a win. I don't want to see you like this and I know you don't want to be like this. What d'ya say?"

He looked at me for the first time. "Fully functional?"

"That's the plan."

"Then get that damn chair and let's go." He pointed to the wheelchair folded up in the corner.

For the first time since I found him, I saw the old fighting spark in his eye.

To meet Hob, I first had to go to the Southern Outpost. I pulled up the small winding road to the checkpoint and was waved through. I didn't have time to park before Meghan met us. She was wearing her green and khaki uniform and had her blond hair pulled back. I rolled down the window as she approached.

"We have a little drive ahead of us," she said, eyeballing Torch in the passenger seat. "Just follow me."

I gave her a nod and turned the truck around. She got in one of the black trucks parked by the checkpoint. I followed her deep into the Elven Nation. After many twists and turns we finally turned onto a well maintained gravel road with a checkpoint at the end of it. It reminded me of the checkpoint at the southern outpost except this one had two buildings and an unknown number of guards protecting it. The barricade was lowered as soon as our trucks were in sight. We didn't even have to slow down; Meg just gave them a little wave out the window as we passed.

We pulled up to an enormous house. It was constructed with large wood beams and windows. I'd never been big on architecture, but I can honestly say this building was beautiful. There was a fountain out front that wasn't on. The grass looked freshly mowed. I could see a few other buildings around the property. The forest had grown up close, giving them heavy shade and obscuring my view. The whole place had an air of reclamation.

We pulled around the fountain and parked. In the center of the fountain an elven woman poured water out of a large jug, at least she would have been pouring if the fountain was working. She had the typical delicate and slender elven features. She wore a long flowing robe and had flowers in her hair. Moss had grown over parts of the fountain. A few inches of stagnant water sat inside.

"This way," Queen Isabelle called.

I realized I had been lost in a kind of daydream. I smiled and got out of the truck. I grabbed the wheelchair out of the back and helped Torch into it. There wasn't a ramp up the stairs to where Isabelle was standing so I hauled Torch up backward. I tried not to jar him too much as the chair rolled from step to step.

When we made it to the top, Isabelle was standing with a servant by the front door. He was around five feet tall, wearing a gray suit and tie. He looked like a butler.

"Obie, this is Bertram," Isabelle said, holding a hand out to the man. "Bertram, this is Obie and Torch. They're friends."

Bertram bowed slightly and gave us a nod. "A pleasure, gentlemen."

"Bertram is in charge of the palace and grounds," Isabelle said. "Hob is waiting for you in the east wing; Bertram will take you to him. If you'll excuse me, I have some business to attend to."

"Thanks," I said.

Bertram bowed as Isabelle passed. When she had disappeared, he turned to us. "This way please."

We followed Bertram down a hallway with double doors at the end. Each door had a carving of an oak tree inside a circle. He opened one of the doors and stood aside for us to enter. On the other side was another hallway. I assumed this was the east wing. We followed him to the library. The walls were lined with bookshelves, neatly filled with old books. There was one section of the library where the shelves were bare. Crates sat on the floor in front of the empty shelves. A fireplace was built into the wall. There was a table and a pair of plush chairs in front of it.

Hob sat on the floor with the crates. I could see they were full of books, but couldn't tell if he was boxing them up or putting them on the shelves.

He stood to greet us. "It is good to see you both. *Willkommen.*"

"What is this place?" I asked, looking around the room.

"It is a library," Hob said without a hint of sarcasm.

"No, I mean the whole palace," I said, waving my hands around in the air. "Where did it come from?"

"It was built by the first Queen," Hob said. "This is the palace of the Elven Nation. It was not used for many years. Bertram did an excellent job maintaining it, although it was too much work for one person."

I nodded. "He must be happy to see it being used again."

"We all are," Hob said.

"Is everything ready?" I asked.

"Please follow," Hob said.

He led us down the hall into a room that was empty except for a sheet-covered table. The sheet had three lumps under it. Hob pulled back the sheet to reveal an arm and two legs molded out of clay. The day before, I had delivered the clay the golems had been made out of to the Southern Outpost. Hob had an elven ceramist mold it into limbs for Torch. I could see magical circles carved into molds.

"Let's get this done already," Torch said, looking at his spare parts on the table.

Hob held up a hand. "Before we start I must say that once the limbs have been connected if you make the change it will break the spell and they will crumble. You must not change from your human form."

"I'd rather have one form than be a cripple in three," he said.

"Then onto the table please," Hob said.

I helped Torch onto the table. He lay on his back.

Hob lined up the arm and legs where they should go. "You must stay very still. Obie, I will need your help. I tested some magic. While it is true we do not need dust, channeling the energy is strenuous. I feel something on this level is more than I can handle on my own. I need you to heal me while I am casting the spell. My hope is that it will be enough."

"Okay," I said. "I'm ready when you are."

Hob held out his hand over Torch. "Begin."

I poured energy into Hob. I could feel it flowing into him and then be directed away like a leaf being washed downstream. Sweat broke out on Hob's forehead and his hands shook from the strain. The limbs attached to Torch and slowly took on the appearance of flesh. It was easy to see where the limbs connected because while they looked like real flesh, they didn't match his dark pigmentation.

Hob's knees started to buckle from the strain. I thought about stopping but didn't know what would happen to him if I did. When Hob finished the spell, he fell forward, catching himself on the edge of the table. He panted trying to catch his breath.

"You okay?"

Hob nodded. "*Ja,* I need a moment."

Torch raised his arm—his new arm. He flexed his hand and turned it, looking at it.

"Well?" I asked. "What d'ya think?"

"It feels weird." He sat up and moved his feet. "Let's try them out."

He eased off the table. He tested his weight on the legs and then took a step. He instantly lost his balance, falling forward but catching himself with his hands.

I grabbed his arm and helped him up. "Everything okay?"

He grinned at me. "Yeah, just figuring out how they handle."

He practiced walking around the room and by the time Hob caught his breath he was walking on his own without too many balance issues.

CHAPTER · 34

"So that's it?" Jarod asked. "Torch got his legs, and all the Keepers just went their separate ways?"

I nodded. "Cearbhall's going to visit his homeland. He's never said anything but I know he's missed it. Mila's taking some time to recover. I don't know what she'll do after that."

The last thing on my to-do list was to take Jarod back to Texas. I'd been filling him in along the way. It's not something I'd normally have done but it didn't seem like keeping it all a secret was that important and he knew half the story anyway. Besides, it was a long drive.

"What about you?" I asked. "What's next in Jarod's story?"

"I'm going to focus on my daughter, Hailey. I took that job to try and give her a better life but I've come to realize that being there for her is the best thing I can do. I'm swearing off questionable high paying jobs. I'll probably go back to truck driving until I can save enough to start a business. I think I want to be my own boss. Maybe a vape shop?"

I didn't know what a vape shop was. It would be one of those things I'd normally ask Holt about. He really kept me up to date.

Jarod pointed ahead. "Second house on the right. The blue one."

I pulled up to a nice looking, two-story.

"Thanks for the ride and not, you know, killing me," Jarod said.

"No problem." I chuckled. "One more thing, open the glovebox. There's an envelope for you."

He took out a manila envelope. "What's this?"

"Open it."

He found a stack of cash. "Holy shit, how much money is this?"

"Enough to start a vape shop . . . I think."

"I can't take your money," Jarod said.

"Sure you can, you just hold onto it and get out of the truck. Don't overthink it."

He was about to protest again when an older couple and a young girl walked out of the house.

"Is that Hailey?" I motioned toward the group.

"Yeah," he said.

"What are you sitting here for? Go."

He got out of the truck. Hailey ran and jumped into his arms. I reached into my pocket and pulled out the stack of postcards. *I would like to see you.* I typed a new address in my phone. When the map came up I backed out of the driveway and gave Jarod a wave as I pulled out. I was already halfway to Vegas. In sixteen hours I'd be there. I was looking forward to a fresh start.

www.authorbenmeeks.com/thank-you

Ben is a North Georgia native, and world traveler, who prides himself on using real world experiences to add realism to his fiction. He was a medal winner in a martial arts competition, been in a high speed car chase, had a late night phone call from the Secret Service, who he hung up on, and been shot. When not writing about himself in the third person he is hard at work writing Contemporary Fantasy and Science Fiction.